Jazzy opened the bathroom door and stepped inside.

Caitlin was right about the smell of barbeque sauce. It was even stronger in here. Odd.

The room was small, with a bathtub instead of a shower stall, and a thick white curtain pulled closed. She grasped the top of the shower curtain and jerked it open.

The persistent odor of barbeque sauce struck her again. Then her heart skidded to a stop. Blood drained from her face.

Now would be a good time to scream. One gathered in her diaphragm, but her throat seemed frozen. Instead of a scream, she barely managed to produce a whimper.

A man lay in the bathtub. Fully clothed. Mouth open. Eyes fixed on the ceiling.

Dead.

Her stomach lurched as she scanned the sticky red stuff covering his body. Not blood. Barbeque sauce. The man's body was covered in barbeque sauce.

Books by Virginia Smith

Love Inspired Suspense

Murder by Mushroom
Bluegrass Peril
A Taste of Murder

VIRGINIA SMITH

A lifelong lover of books, Virginia Smith has always enjoyed immersing herself in fiction. In her midtwenties she wrote her first story and discovered that writing well is harder than it looks; it took many years to produce a book worthy of publication. During the daylight hours she steadily climbed the corporate ladder and stole time late at night after the kids were in bed to write. With the publication of her first novel, she left her twenty-year corporate profession to devote her energy to her passion—writing stories that honor God and bring a smile to the faces of her readers. When she isn't writing, Ginny and her husband, Ted, enjoy exploring the extremes of nature—snow skiing in the mountains of Utah, motorcycle riding on the curvy roads of central Kentucky, and scuba diving in the warm waters of the Caribbean. Visit www.VirginiaSmith.org.

a TASTE *of* MURDER

VIRGINIA SMITH

Steeple Hill®

Published by Steeple Hill Books™

Steeple Hill®

STEEPLE HILL BOOKS

ISBN-13: 978-0-373-44311-6
ISBN-10: 0-373-44311-0

A TASTE OF MURDER

This edition published by arrangement with Steeple Hill Books.

www.SteepleHill.com

Printed in U.S.A.

It is good to praise the Lord and make music
to your name, O Most High.

—*Psalms* 92:1

In memory of Larry Kirk, and my dear friend Trudy Kirk. You were both with me for my first Bar-B-Q Festival, so every word of this book was written with you in mind.

Larry, I hope you and Jesus are enjoying the story in heaven.

Acknowledgments

I'm so grateful to the people who helped me take this story from idea to finished product. Thanks to:

My incredible husband, Ted, for taking me to the Owensboro Bar-B-Q Festival, and for telling me about hunting dogs.

My father, Myron Patrick, for taking me hunting and fishing when I was a kid, and for Old Sue.

The faculty and students of Franklin County High School, for allowing me the honor of judging their Miss FCHS pageant, and for inviting me to speak to their English classes. (Go Flyers!)

Jill Elizabeth Nelson and Tracy Ruckman for expert critiques and advice that made this story better.

The CWFI Critique Group, for helping me work out the plot: Amy Barkman, Dr. Richard Leonard, Ann Knowles, Vicki Tiede, Sherry Kyle, Tracy Ruckman and Amy Smith. They're talented writers themselves, and I'm privileged to know them.

My agent and friend, Wendy Lawton, for her unfailing support and encouragement.

All the folks at Steeple Hill, especially Krista Stroever and Louise Rozett, for being so good at what they do.

And finally, thanks to my Lord Jesus, for everything. Absolutely everything.

PROLOGUE

The fire door closed behind him with a thud. Silence pressed against Josh Kirkland's eardrums in the hotel's back stairwell, ringing inside his head after the hubbub of the lobby. He started to climb, the echo of his footsteps an oddly welcome disruption of the noiseless space that surrounded him.

At the landing on the third floor, he paused to catch his breath. His heart pounded against his ribs, a sure sign that he needed to spend more time on the treadmill at the gym. He was panting like an old dog in the summertime after just a couple flights of stairs.

A sound reverberated from above. The click of a door being quietly shut. Josh smiled. She was probably checking on him, making sure he was on his way. He fished the magnetic card out of his pocket, a yellow sticky note still clinging to the side of it.

> Can we talk about your vote? Meet me in room 4057 during your lunch break. Come up the back stairs so nobody sees. I'll make it worth your while.

No signature, but that didn't much matter to him. He'd thought about it all morning, and finally decided that it must have been written by one of the pageant contestants. His pulse accelerated as he remembered a few of the beautiful young women last year parading past the judges' table in their evening gowns.

Or maybe it was one of the mothers of the younger contestants. Some of those women were among the most overbearing human beings on the planet. After last year's pageant he'd gotten some pretty nasty e-mails from mothers of girls who didn't win. On the other hand, a few of those women would go to amazing lengths to ensure their daughters took home the title of Little Princess. Including emptying their checking accounts for a little "title insurance."

He bounded up the stairs to the fourth floor. At the top he opened the fire door slowly and peeked through. The hallway was deserted. He slipped across the thick carpet to the room with the numbers 4057 on the door.

Inside, he leaned against the closed door and looked around. Doubt tickled at his mind. Something wasn't right.

"Hello?"

No answer. He stepped forward, glancing into the dark bathroom as he passed. Empty.

The room looked as though it had just been cleaned. Beds made. Carpet swept. Fresh notepad and pen beside the phone on the desk.

Only one thing looked out of place. A white grocery sack on the dresser. He moved closer. It was full, like somebody had been shopping. He peered inside.

Uh-oh. Maybe he was wrong. There were at least half a dozen bottles of—

A movement in the mirror above the dresser caught his eye. Every muscle in his body tensed as the door to the adjoining room swung open.

Tension fled, replaced by irritation as he recognized the person who stepped into view.

"What's going on here?" He gestured toward the bag. "Is this your idea of a joke?"

His gaze dropped to watch in the mirror as the gloved hands, holding a thick rope, rose. Uncomprehending, he locked gazes with the reflection.

The rope was around his neck before he could move.

ONE

"What in the world have you gotten us into, Jasmine Delaney?"

Jazzy bit back a groan as she stared into the wide-eyed face of her friend. Liz clutched her cello case to her chest. A girl around ten years old—one of the horde that filled the hotel lobby—brushed past her in hot pursuit of a giggling friend.

Shaking her head, Jazzy followed the girls' progress as they threaded through the line of hotel guests waiting to check in. A room-service waiter with a tray of covered dishes balanced over his head barely avoided disaster when they dashed by him. They narrowly missed a repairman before disappearing behind the elevators.

With an apologetic grimace, Jazzy faced her friend. "When the bride gave me the reservation number she did mention that I was getting one of the few remaining rooms." A shriek of high-pitched laughter from a group of girls seated on nearby sofas pierced the din. Jazzy winced. "I assumed the rooms were taken by people attending the Bar-B-Q Festival. I had no idea there would be so many children."

"Smile!" The third member of their trio pointed a digital camera in their faces for the fifth time in as many minutes. A confirmed scrapbooker, Caitlin was forever snapping pictures of their part-time ensemble during rehearsals and performances. It drove Jazzy crazy.

Nevertheless, she put her head close to Liz's and pasted on a cheesy grin. The urge to hold bunny fingers above her grouchy friend's head was strong, but she resisted.

Caitlin lowered the camera, frowning. "Darn. I think the batteries just died."

"Here, let me." Jazzy whipped out her cell phone, pointed and caught a shot of Caitlin scowling at her camera.

Liz glared as another group of giggling girls brushed by them a little too close. "What's with all these kids?"

The line moved forward. A tall woman pushed by Jazzy and marched to the front of the line. Jazzy exchanged a glance with Caitlin, who shrugged and bent to drag her gigantic duffel bag into place behind her.

Straightening, Caitlin gestured with her flute case to a point behind Jazzy's head. "That's why. Look what's going on in this hotel tomorrow."

Jazzy turned her head in the direction Caitlin indicated. A poster on a marquee near the edge of the reception desk detailed Waynesboro Barbecue Festival Events. She scanned the entries until she spotted the one to which Caitlin referred. A baby pageant would be held in the International Ballroom tomorrow morning, followed by the Toddler Pageant, the Youth Pageant, the Little Princess Pageant and the Miss Bar-B-Q Teen Pageant. The biggest event, the crowning of Miss Bar-B-Q Festival, would be held at eight-thirty tomorrow night.

Jazzy groaned out loud this time. They'd reserved a room smack-dab in the middle of beauty pageant central.

Liz clutched the cello case tighter. "Do you suppose we could find another hotel?" Strands of her dark hair took on a life of their own as she whipped her head to watch a harried mother herd a brood of towheaded children toward the lobby restaurant.

Jazzy wished they could. So far the Executive Inn wasn't living up to its name. She'd expected something far newer, but judging by the worn carpet and slightly shabby state of the wingback chairs grouped to form conversation nooks throughout the lobby, this hotel had been around for a while. She examined the gleaming glass front doors with a critical eye. At least they looked clean.

"I doubt it. The bride made this reservation months ago. Waynesboro isn't a very big town to begin with, and the festival seems to have commandeered every available room." Jazzy looked at her watch. "Besides, we don't have time. We've got to be at the church for the rehearsal in ninety minutes."

"Oh, c'mon." Caitlin punched Liz on the arm, grinning. "Don't be a Scrooge. You like kids, don't you?"

"Singly," Liz replied instantly. "And preferably sleeping."

As another loud burst of laughter rose from the girls on the sofa, Jazzy had to agree. Raised as an only child, she'd never been comfortable with large groups of kids. Except, of course, when she was playing in the school orchestra or the junior symphony. But then everybody was governed by the rules of the music—every note, every beat carefully orchestrated by the conductor.

"I told you on the phone we needed a room on the second floor in *this* wing." The voice cut through the general din of the lobby. "I ain't gonna have my daughter traipsing from the backside of the hotel in her fancy clothes tomorrow afternoon."

The broad-shouldered woman who had barged past them stood before the high counter, her anger evident in her white-fingered grip on the straps of a blue canvas handbag. A girl around ten or eleven years old stood quietly beside her, head bowed. Jazzy caught a quick glimpse of a blush-stained cheek before the girl sidled away from the woman, stopping nearby but facing in the opposite direction as though trying to disassociate herself from the argument that was beginning to attract attention. Jazzy exchanged a glance with Liz, eyebrows arched.

The desk clerk, a young man with an imperturbable expression, issued a response in a low voice, which Jazzy couldn't distinguish.

"I don't care if you're full. Move somebody. I made these reservations eight months ago, and I told you on the phone where I wanted our room."

The young man mumbled something else without looking up as he tapped on a keyboard. Apparently his words served only to enrage the woman.

"I don't know who I talked to, but that shouldn't make no never-mind. Don't you have a place in that computer to record customer requests?" She pounded a finger on the top of the monitor in front of the clerk.

Another guest walked away from the opposite end of the counter, and the teenage girl seated behind an identical monitor caught Jazzy's eye. "I can help whoever's next."

Her rolling suitcase in one hand and her violin case in the other, Jazzy stepped up to the counter. Liz and Caitlin followed behind her.

"I have a reservation," she said. "The name's Jasmine Delaney."

The girl's fingers flew across the keyboard, her eyes fixed on the screen in front of her. "For an economy double?"

"That's right. But if you have a rollaway, there will be three of us in the room."

The other desk clerk got out of his chair to swipe a key card through the encoder that rested on the counter between the two monitors. Jazzy saw him exchange a quick eye-roll with the girl checking her in.

The girl awarded him a sympathetic grimace before returning her attention to Jazzy. "Sorry, but they're all gone. Will two double beds be okay?"

Jazzy glanced at her friends. She supposed she could double up with one of them. The three had played together for over a year, but this was their first overnight gig. It might be a test of their friendship.

"Sure, that'll be fine."

"Names of the other two guests?"

"Liz Carmichael and Caitlin Saylor."

The girl's nimble fingers recorded their names into the computer, then without looking up she said, "The room's been paid for, but I need to see an ID."

As Jazzy dug her wallet out of her purse, the angry guest at the other end of the counter walked past, her embarrassed daughter in tow. The girl shuffled behind with her head bowed, limp brown hair falling forward to hide her features. Judging from the satisfied expression on the woman's broad face, she'd gotten her way with the room.

"Do you want three keys?"

Jazzy glanced at Liz.

"Definitely."

The desk clerk rolled her chair sideways toward the key encoder. She punched some buttons, paused with a glance toward the young man, punched some more then swiped three cards.

Room keys in hand, Jazzy and her friends gathered their various bags and instrument cases and headed toward the elevator. On the fourth floor they followed the hallway around an open-air atrium. From there Jazzy could see the extent of the lobby. The place might be old, but the owners had done a good job with the decor. A trio of gigantic Florida palms towered from a huge planter in the center, standing guard over the entrance to the restaurant. In the other corner a neon sign announced the location of the Time Out Lounge, and in front of that a series of cubicles contained the hotel's business center.

"Look at that." Caitlin dipped her head toward one of the front cubicles. "There's a radio station right here in the lobby."

Jazzy read a sign above an empty desk loaded with all kinds of fancy equipment. "WKBR Country Radio." Her lips twisted. "I'll bet they never heard of Haydn."

Liz laughed as they rounded a corner. "Don't be such a music snob, Jazzy."

They wound away from the atrium, turned at another corridor and walked down the long hallway. Theirs was the second room from the end. Jazzy dropped her suitcase as she pulled a key card out of its paper sleeve.

"I hope these walls are soundproof." Liz leveled a glare at the closed door next to theirs. "With my luck we'll have a ton of those pint-sized beauty pageant contestants right next door.

"It'll be okay," Caitlin said. "It's only for a couple of nights." She shifted her glance to Jazzy. "How did you find out about this wedding gig, anyway? And how come they had to bring us all the way from Lexington? Couldn't they get a local ensemble to play?"

Jazzy shook her head as she swiped the card through the reader on the door. "I guess the Bar-B-Q Festival takes priority with the local groups. The bride's brother read about our ensemble on my ShoutLife profile. He sent a note asking if we'd be willing to make the drive down to Waynesboro. I figured since they're willing to pay us and cover our hotel bill, it would be worth the trip."

The light on the door turned green, and Jazzy pushed down on the handle. She didn't see any need to mention the fact that Derrick Rogers's profile picture on the online community ShoutLife identified him as a drop-dead gorgeous guy just about her age. And proclaimed that he was a Christian. The combination had been too good to pass up.

"I can't imagine why someone would plan a wedding on a weekend when their town is going to be overflowing with out-of-town barbecue lovers." Liz's lips pursed. "That's poor planning, if you ask me."

"Oh, come on, Liz." Caitlin pushed past Jazzy into the room. "Quit acting like you're going to a funeral. We're gonna have fun. I searched the Internet on this festival thing and read up on it. It's a big deal, with a bunch of different contests for barbecue and burgoo. All kinds of people come to it, and the barbecue teams cook for days in advance. Apparently the food is awesome." She inhaled deeply. "Wow, I can already smell the barbecue sauce."

Liz wrinkled her nose as she, too, pushed into the room. "What is burgoo?"

Jazzy grinned at her. "Your Oregon roots are showing. Every good Kentuckian knows what burgoo is."

"It's sort of a stew," Caitlin explained. "It's made with several different kinds of meat and vegetables and spices. People in Kentucky, especially in mountains and small towns like Waynesboro, are as proud of their secret burgoo recipes as Texans are of their chili recipes."

"I like chili." Liz tossed her suitcase on a bed. "What kind of meat's in burgoo?"

Jazzy followed them inside, past the closed bathroom door. "Well, here's what an old guy from eastern Kentucky told me when I asked that question." She affected a hillbilly drawl. "Hit's got whatever roadkill we pick up 'at day. Coon. Squirrel. Possum burgoo makes good eatin', long as it ain't bin layin' there more'n a day or two."

Liz's mouth twisted. "That is disgusting."

Jazzy laughed and bumped Liz with her violin case. "I'm kidding, girl. Don't be so gullible. It's made from lamb, chicken and pork."

Liz could be a bit on the sour side, but she was an excellent cellist, and a good friend. Jazzy swiveled to survey the room. Decent-sized, with two double beds, an armoire with a television set and a writing desk near the window. She lifted the floral bedspread and inspected the sheets. They smelled a little stale, but looked clean.

Caitlin was watching with an amused expression. "Well, Miss Clean Freak?"

"Acceptable," she said as she dropped her violin case onto the mattress. Liz had claimed the other bed, which was okay with her. She liked being nearest the bathroom.

"Not bad." Liz opened a drawer in the nightstand and peered inside. "The Gideons have been here."

Caitlin collapsed onto the bed. She looked up at Jazzy. "Are there enough towels? I wouldn't mind grabbing a shower before the rehearsal."

"I'll check."

Jazzy hefted her suitcase up on the mattress beside her violin and turned toward the bathroom.

"And see if there are three soaps," Liz added. "No offense, girls, but I want my own."

Jazzy opened the bathroom door and stepped inside. Caitlin was right about the smell of barbecue sauce. It was even stronger in here. Odd. Maybe the bathroom was vented to draw air from outside, where the contestants would be cooking their festival entries.

The room was small, with a bathtub instead of a shower stall, and a thick white curtain pulled closed. The white fixtures sparkled, thank goodness. She counted four towels and four washcloths, but only one small cake of soap. There might be another in the bathtub soap dish, though.

She grasped the top of the shower curtain and jerked it open. Rings slid across the rod with a metallic scrape.

The strong odor of barbecue sauce slapped her in the face. At the same time, her heart skidded to a stop. Blood drained from her face, leaving her cheeks clammy.

Now would be a good time to scream. One gathered in her diaphragm, but her throat seemed frozen. Instead of a scream, she barely managed to produce a whimper.

A man lay in the bathtub. Fully clothed. Mouth open. Eyes fixed on the ceiling. Tongue hanging grotesquely out.

Dead.

Her stomach lurched as she scanned the sticky red stuff covering his body. Blood?

She placed a hand over her mouth and swallowed back a sudden surge of acid.

Not blood. Barbecue sauce. The man's body was covered in barbecue sauce.

TWO

Derrick pulled his pickup beneath the covered entryway to the Executive Inn. Though today was only Thursday, the parking lot was already full. If the ensemble ladies had been lucky enough to find a parking space in the hotel's lot, they'd better ride to the church with him. That way they could leave their car parked until they were ready to go home. Since the Executive Inn marked the western end of the festival route, finding an empty parking space within miles of the place before Sunday afternoon would be nearly impossible.

Of course, they could have easily walked the three blocks to the church. But he figured they'd be lugging instrument cases and music stands and what-have-you. Plus, he wanted an opportunity to welcome them to town before they got swept into the wedding chaos.

He stopped the pickup and peered through the glass doors for three musicians who, hopefully, were watching for him. When nobody emerged, he pulled the pickup forward and over to the yellow-painted curb behind three deputy sheriff vehicles.

"Hey, you can't park there." The teenage parking attendant removed an earbud from his ear and punched a button on his iPod when Derrick got out and slammed the door. "That's a tow zone."

Derrick kept walking toward the door. "Yeah, well I wouldn't call the tow truck if I was you. I'm here to pick up the musicians who'll be playing at the sheriff's son's wedding tomorrow. We don't want them to be late for the rehearsal, now, do we?" He winked at the kid to take the sting out of his words.

The guy blanched. "Uh, no, sir, we sure don't." Apparently he was familiar with Sheriff Maguire.

Derrick grinned. The sheriff was well known among the local teenagers. And they all sincerely hoped they were not well known to Sheriff Maguire.

"What's with the cop cars?" He pointed toward the trio lined along the curb.

The kid shrugged and replaced the earbud.

Derrick glanced up the street, where a crew was hard at work setting up a bunch of carnival rides in the grassy lot in front of the American Legion building. Smoke from the nearest barbecue crew's pit billowed toward them and filled the air with the smell of burning hickory. A merry-go-round and a small Ferris wheel were already in place, and the men were tightening bolts on the curved red seats of another ride. Derrick shook his head. Barbecue and a Tilt-A-Whirl. What a combination.

He stepped from the humid Kentucky spring heat through a cold blast of air-conditioned wind rushing from the hotel lobby. The place was packed, as he knew it would be. They were expecting more than ten thousand festival-goers this year, and every hotel in town had been sold out for months. Chelsea had been lucky to snag the last few rooms for the wedding guests and out-of-town relatives who hadn't planned ahead. Of course, the fact that she was marrying the son of one of Waynesboro's most prominent citizens might have helped a bit. The hotel management was eager to keep her happy.

Derrick stood in the lobby, looking around for three young women with musical instruments. Odd. He frowned down at his watch. Why weren't they down here waiting for him? They were supposed to be at the church in fifteen minutes.

Ignoring the line of people waiting to check in, he approached the front desk when a guest walked away clutching a magnetic key card. The clerk looked up, an unspoken query on his face.

"Could you ring a guest's room for me?" He leaned an arm on the high counter. "Miss Jasmine Delaney."

The young man's mouth gaped, and his gaze flickered toward the line of guests waiting to check in. "Uh, she's not in her room."

"She's not?" Derrick cocked his head at the guy. "Hasn't she checked in?"

He gave a quick nod. "Yes, sir, about an hour ago. But there were some, uh, some problems." He lowered his voice and caught Derrick's gaze. "She's being questioned by the police right now."

"The police?" Derrick couldn't help it. Surprise made his voice carry through the lobby.

The kid's eyes flicked sideways again. "Yes, sir. But we're supposed to keep it quiet because of, you know." He nodded toward the line of guests. "The boss doesn't want anyone to panic."

"But what has she done?" Derrick's thoughts whirled as he tried to conjure a picture of the girl's ShoutLife profile. She had looked safe enough. Her blog posts openly proclaimed her Christian beliefs and her passion for music. Of course, most of the people she listed as her favorites were complete unknowns to Derrick. He barely knew a flute from a tuba.

"I don't know." The clerk's voice lowered even more. Derrick had to lean over the counter to catch his words. "But I heard somebody's been murdered."

Derrick reared back. *Murdered? Oh, great. Terrific.* His little sister was supposed to get married in less than twenty-four hours, and her musicians were being arrested for murder. And to make matters worse, he was the one who'd hired them.

Sheriff Maguire was going to throw a fit.

"Listen, I need to talk to the deputy in charge," he said. "Miss Delaney's ensemble is supposed to play at my sister's wedding tomorrow. In fact, I'm supposed to have them at the rehearsal in—" he glanced at his watch "—ten minutes."

The young man considered him for less than a second. "They're in the Governor's Room, just past the restrooms."

Derrick strode through the lobby in the direction the young man indicated. He weaved around a cluster of people huddled before a festival event marquee and passed the ladies' lounge. The hallway beyond contained several meeting rooms, the doors all closed. He found the one labeled Governor's Room and entered without knocking.

The people inside sat in chairs around a conference table, two men in uniform and three women. Everyone's attention seemed to be focused on the young woman at the end, the one he immediately recognized from the photos he'd studied online. Jasmine Delaney. He'd spent enough time examining images of her face, with its pixie chin and arresting green eyes, to pick her out in a crowd. She looked very different at the moment, though, with a red nose and eyes puffy from crying. A box of tissues sat on the table, and several crumpled-up white wads littered the surface before her.

She looked up at him when he came into the room, and their eyes met. Something surged between them, and the shock of it glued Derrick's feet to the carpet. For a moment he couldn't look anywhere but at her. In that instant he knew that this girl was not guilty of murder.

A wave of relief washed over him, mixed with something

else. Compassion, maybe? The poor girl looked fragile, almost frail, and absolutely terrified.

One of the deputies rose and took a step toward him. "I'm sorry, sir, but you can't come in here."

"Fine." Derrick tore his gaze from the girl's. He unclipped the cell phone from his belt and held it toward the man. "But could you do me a favor? Call Sheriff Maguire and explain why I'm not at his son's wedding rehearsal with the musicians."

The deputy stared at the phone, suddenly hesitant.

"'Lo, Derrick." Matt Farmer, the deputy on the other side of the table, nodded. They'd known each other for years, had grown up in the same neighborhood. "We're just about finished here. I don't see any reason we can't release these ladies and let them get on to the rehearsal. You got anything else, Frank?"

The other deputy directed his words toward Jasmine. "Yeah, I want to hear about that electrician one more time."

Her lips tightened before she answered. Good. A show of spunk meant she wasn't one of those women who collapsed into an emotional heap under stress.

She caught Frank in an unflinching stare. "I've told you at least a dozen times in the last hour and a half—I don't know if he was an electrician, or a repairman, or what. He did have a long gray ponytail sticking out of the back of his cap, but other than that I barely noticed him. I was watching two little girls who almost ran right into a waiter with a full tray in his hands."

"And the reason you first called him a repairman is…"

Jasmine blew an impatient breath. "Because he was wearing a gray shirt that might have been a uniform, and he was carrying a beat-up duffel bag that looked like it might have tools in it. But it was just an impression. I saw him from behind. For all I know he was a guest checking into the hotel and he has cheap luggage."

"But he was heading toward the door. You're sure of that?"

She slapped a hand down on the table. "No, I'm not! I think he was heading for the door, but he might just as easily have been going toward the elevator, or even toward the lounge. I didn't see him go outside. I wasn't watching him."

Definitely not the collapsing kind. Instead, this girl looked like she had a temper packed with dynamite, and the deputy's match was getting a little too close.

Derrick stepped forward. "We really need to get going. I'm sure if these ladies remember anything else, they'll tell it to Sheriff Maguire. He's at the rehearsal right now."

Matt shook his head. "The Sheriff is out trying to find the victim's next of kin at the moment."

"Okay, then they'll call you if they have anything else to say. And you know where to find them."

Matt stared at him a moment before lifting a shoulder. "I'm sure we'll have more questions later."

The look of gratitude Jazzy shot Derrick made him stand a bit taller.

The young woman on Jasmine's left rose from her seat, her near six-foot frame towering above Frank. She was broomstick-thin, a striking contrast to the heavy blonde across the table, who also stood.

"Come on, Jazzy." The tall brunette shoved her chair under the table.

"You sure you're up to it, honey?" The blonde hefted the strap of a purse onto her shoulder, eyeing Jasmine with concern etched in her brow. "You had quite a shock up there."

Jazzy's throat convulsed as her troubled gaze moved from the brunette to her other friend. Whatever shock she'd experienced was going to haunt her for a while. He itched to ask what had happened, but they were running so late. He'd give Matt a call later and pry the information out of him.

"'Course she's up to it." The other girl put an arm around Jasmine's shoulders and gave a squeeze. "Jazzy's a professional. We signed on for a job, and we're going to do it. Right?"

Jasmine's lips formed a trembling smile and she nodded. "Right." She lifted her chin, and then turned toward him. "Derrick Rogers? I'm Jasmine Delaney."

As if he didn't know that. Her hand felt warm in his, and soft. "Nice to meet you, Miss Delaney."

"Please call me Jasmine. Or Jazzy. And these are my friends, Liz and Caitlin."

Jazzy. He'd noticed the nickname mentioned in a couple of the comments on her ShoutLife profile, and now that he'd seen her in person, he decided it suited her. This woman deserved a name with some spunk.

He shook each lady's hand, then glanced at his watch. "We're going to be late, but not too bad. I'll call my sister while you grab your instruments and whatever else you need. I'm parked right out front."

Jazzy had been stooping to pick up a handbag from the floor, and froze. Straightening, she looked at Matt. "Our instruments are upstairs, in with…" Her voice trembled.

"I'll get them." Frank stepped toward the door, then stopped and caught Jazzy in a stare. "On second thought, I'll take you to the church myself. I want to hear you go over it one more time."

He disappeared through the door as Jazzy sucked in an outraged breath. Derrick exchanged a glance with Matt, who shrugged. Apparently Matt wasn't willing to cross his partner when it came to questioning witnesses.

Liz rushed across the room and stuck her head out the door. "I need my bag, too," she called after the deputy. "It has my music portfolio in it."

Jazzy turned to Matt. "What will happen to the rest of our stuff?"

"Yeah," said Caitlin, "and where will we stay? We heard the hotel is full, and I am not going back into that room. I don't care how much they scrub it."

Derrick saw Jazzy give a delicate shudder. "Me, neither."

Matt shook his head. "I don't know. We're going to have to seal off that room, and probably the ones around it, too. Maybe they'll have some cancellations or something. I'll talk to the manager."

Derrick spoke up. "What happened, exactly?" He directed his question to Matt, but Liz answered.

"There was a dead body in our room when we checked in." She crossed her arms, her mouth a hard line. "Jazzy found it."

Ah. That had to be awful. No wonder she looked shaken up. "Any idea how the guy died? The desk clerk said something about a murder."

Matt nodded. "No doubt about that. Looked to me like he was strangled. And you'll never believe who it was, either."

The muscles in Derrick's stomach knotted. "Somebody I know?"

The deputy nodded. "Everybody knows him. It was Josh Kirkland."

Derrick gave a low whistle. Kirkland was a DJ for the local country radio station, something of a celebrity in town, so of course he'd met the guy. But he didn't know him well. Still… "Right before the festival. Man, that's going to come as a shock to a lot of people."

"You ain't kidding."

Derrick turned to the three musicians. "If the manager doesn't have a place for you to stay, you're welcome to my apartment. It's not very big, and there's only one bed, but it might be the best you can hope for this weekend. I can stay at my mom's for the night."

Jazzy looked up at him, a smile hovering at the edges of her mouth. "That's a very nice offer. Thank you."

He would give up a lot more than his apartment to see that smile break free. Looking down into her eyes, he cleared his throat. "No problem."

THREE

Jazzy and her friends left the obstinate deputy outside the church in his cruiser and trooped inside single-file behind Derrick. The wedding coordinator stood at the front of the sanctuary going over the order of events for a group seated in the first few pews. Her voice echoed off the arched ceiling and the tall, thick-paned windows that lined both sides. How did the woman have the nerve to disturb the reverent stillness of the place? Jazzy found herself tiptoeing up the center aisle.

"Sorry we're late." Derrick directed his apology to the coordinator.

A young woman rose from the front row and approached him. She threw her arms around his neck, standing on tiptoe to do so. "Where have you been? You know I can't do this without my big brother."

The bride. Clear family resemblance. Same sandy blond hair, same oval face. The girl even smiled like her brother, wide and with lots of white teeth in evidence.

A young man, presumably the groom, got up and followed her into the aisle. "I wondered if you got caught up in the mess at the hotel. Dad got a call and ran out of here about twenty minutes ago, saying someone had been killed over there."

"Yeah. In fact, your musicians found the body. That's why we're late."

Gasps reverberated around the sanctuary, and a blush began to tingle in Jazzy's cheeks. Was everyone staring at her?

The bride rushed forward to grab her free hand. "I'm Chelsea Rogers, and this is my fiancé, Quinn Maguire. I'm so sorry! How awful for you, and after you drove all this way to play at our wedding."

Jazzy managed a smile and squeezed her hand before releasing it.

"Quinn's father is the sheriff here," Derrick explained, "so that's why they called him. I'm sure you'll be talking with Sheriff Maguire before this thing is over."

"Terrific," mumbled Liz. She stood behind Jazzy, both hands full with her cello case and a music bag. Liz's expression had assumed its habitual sulk, but Jazzy detected strain in the muscles around her friend's mouth.

She's been affected by the ordeal more than she's letting on.

And no wonder. Jazzy suppressed a shudder as an image of the dead man loomed in her mind. Would that sight ever cease to haunt her?

The wedding coordinator quick-stepped down the aisle. "I hate to seem callous, but we're a little pressed for time. I've got to leave in forty-five minutes."

Thankful to have something besides a corpse to focus on, Jazzy nodded. "Just show us where you want us, and we can be ready in a few minutes."

"Oh, good. Come right up here. I'm Emily, by the way."

Jazzy followed her to a corner of the dais, Caitlin and Liz trailing behind. Three chairs had already been set in front of a grand piano which, judging by its off-centered location, had been pushed back to make room for them.

Emily outlined her instructions as they set down their instrument cases. "From here you should be able to see me in the narthex. I'll signal for you to begin playing at five-thirty as the guests are being seated. Then, when we're ready to begin the ceremony, I'll give you a nod." She peered at the three of them in turn. "You've played weddings before, I hope?"

Jazzy nodded. "Quite a few."

Relief brought a smile to her face. "Oh, good. What piece did you and Chelsea settle on for the processional?"

"She told me to do whatever we wanted," Jazzy replied. "We selected a Handel aria."

Emily grinned. "That will be perfect. Why don't you go ahead and get tuned or whatever you need to do, and we'll be ready in a minute."

She returned to the wedding party, and Caitlin arranged their chairs in the semicircle they preferred while Liz set her cello case on the floor and set up her music stand.

As Jazzy settled in her chair, the fine hair at the base of her skull prickled. Creepy. She almost felt like someone was watching her.

Don't be silly. A dozen people might be watching. They're all sitting in pews, staring this way.

She cast a quick backward glance, but saw nothing except the empty choir loft. Rubbing the tickle away, she let her gaze sweep the sanctuary. Every eye seemed fixed on Emily as the wedding party listened attentively to her instructions about the order of the bridesmaids. Nobody was watching Jazzy, certainly not with a sinister stare.

Sinister?

Where had that come from? Of course nobody was glaring at her with evil intent. Why would they? It was just the old demons raising their heads to torment her.

Still, her muscles remained rigid. As she opened her case and lifted her instrument from the velvet lining, she couldn't help peering at the wedding party, trying to catch one of them glaring at her.

"Are you okay, Jazzy?"

She looked around to find Caitlin watching her closely as she fit the final section of her flute in place.

"I'm fine. Why?"

Caitlin shrugged. "You seem a little jumpy, that's all."

Liz spread her sheet music on the stand and snorted. "You think? I'd be a screaming lunatic if I'd found a dead body in a bathtub." She shuddered. "I may never take a bath again."

Jazzy closed the latches on her violin case quietly. "I am a little spooked," she admitted. "I keep wanting to look over my shoulder, you know? Trying to catch somebody watching me."

"Well..." Caitlin stepped around the center chair and seated herself, a worried expression on her normally cheery face. "There *is* a murderer running around town. I have to admit, I'm not feeling all that comfortable myself."

"Oh, hogwash." Liz positioned her cello between her knees. "You heard the cops. That guy was a local big shot. He probably got on some country boy's bad side, and Bubba did him in. The killer is no threat to three out-of-town musicians. We're perfectly safe."

Jazzy wanted to accept Liz's no-nonsense logic. But why couldn't she shake the feeling that something was wrong, that somebody was watching?

Moving shadows at the side of the church drew her attention, and she gave a startled laugh. Her friends looked up.

"No wonder I feel like somebody's watching me. Look at that."

She nodded toward the thick panes of crystal-cut glass

lining one long side of the sanctuary. No doubt on Sunday mornings the sunlight shining through those panes sent prisms of light dancing over the worshippers, but right now the windows were darkened with the silhouettes of passersby on the sidewalk—dozens of them. Several faces pressed close to the glass to see inside, most of them at child height. Jazzy caught a glimpse of several adults standing close enough to gawk at the activity inside the sanctuary, too.

Liz groaned. "More kids. Is the average age in this town like twelve or something?"

Caitlin laughed at her. "I'll bet they're some of the same kids we saw at the hotel. We're only a few blocks away, and the street outside is part of the festival route. They're probably out with their mothers getting the lay of the land."

"Okay, let's head out to the narthex." Emily's voice cut into their conversation. "We need to run through it from the top."

Jazzy straightened in her chair. "Oops. We'd better get tuned."

She positioned her violin and played an A. Having perfect pitch definitely helped in the tuning process, but at times the gift felt more like a curse. Especially when she attended her cousin's middle-school band concerts. Caitlin and Liz tuned their instruments to match her tone. After a few minor adjustments, they were ready to begin.

Caitlin gave the count with a subtle nod. Jazzy's and Liz's feet caught the pace for their selected number, Handel's famous "Air for Water Music." They came in together with the ease of many hours of practice. This was one of Jazzy's favorites, and she closed her eyes to let the music wash over her. Thoughts of bodies and murderers and possible sinister watchers faded as she gave herself over to the intricate harmonies of the piece.

The processional progressed until the bridal party was lined up at the front of the sanctuary. Then the doors at the back closed, and after an appropriately dramatic pause, Caitlin cued them to launch into the bridal march. This time Jazzy kept her eyes open. When the doors parted to reveal Chelsea standing there, arm-in-arm with Derrick, she felt a tickle at the back of her eyes.

She was such a sap. No matter how many times she played this, the music still made her cry.

Standing at the entrance to the sanctuary, Derrick placed his left hand over Chelsea's on his arm, and squeezed. The grin she directed up at him melted his heart. This whole wedding thing had seemed so unreal until now. Lots of talk and plans and Mom's house stuffed full of doodads made out of pink satin and white lace. But that music had a way of jerking a guy into reality. This was really happening. His kid sister was about to marry the love of her life.

"Okay," Emily said. "Walk real slow. Step, pause, step, pause."

They started down the aisle, and Derrick noticed that Mom, standing in her place in the front pew, was dabbing at her eyes with a tissue. She'd be all alone when Chelsea moved out. He'd have to make sure to stop by the house more often to keep her company. Let her feed him home-cooked meals. Encourage her to get out more, too.

"They're really good, aren't they?" Chelsea whispered. "I'm glad you found them."

She was staring ahead. Derrick looked that way and caught sight of Jazzy. No longer puffy with tears, her eyes seemed dreamy now, and her smile tender. Her body swayed with the music, her arm moving smoothly as she drew her bow across the strings of her fiddle. She handled the thing like it was an extension of herself.

She wasn't married, or at least her online profile stated that she was single. Was she seeing anybody? He'd looked through her blog posts and hadn't seen any mention of a boyfriend. A bunch of guys on her friends list, but what pretty girl with gorgeous green eyes wouldn't have a ton of guys sending her Friend invites?

"Yes," he managed. "They are good."

Step, pause. Step, pause.

"Oh, good. Mr. Kirkland just got here." Chelsea nodded toward a pew in the front. "He's here to find out how we want the chairs and stuff set up for the reception. I wonder if Mom saw him."

"Kirkland?" Startled, Derrick looked where Chelsea indicated. A fiftyish guy with short, silver-streaked dark hair had just entered and chosen a seat on the far side of a pew in the center of the sanctuary, watching the musicians. Josh Kirkland's brother. Obviously he had not yet been informed of his brother's fate. "What's he doing here?"

Chelsea shrugged. "The regular groundskeeper is on vacation. Reverend Evans heard that Mr. Kirkland does this sort of work for the hotel all the time, so he hired him to fill in."

Derrick hesitated. The guy needed to be told about his brother, but Derrick didn't think such terrible news should come from him. They were nearing the front of the sanctuary, where Quinn and Reverend Evans stood waiting, when they heard a commotion behind them. Loud static from a two-way radio cut through the music, and Derrick turned to see Sheriff Maguire stride through the doorway, the various tools of his trade jingling on his police belt. His head swiveled as he looked around the sanctuary, and then his gaze settled on Les Kirkland.

"Thank goodness." Derrick was off the hook. The sheriff was far more qualified to deliver the news.

"What's going on, Derrick?" Chelsea asked.

He squeezed her hand hard against the bad news he was

about to deliver. "That guy who was killed over at the Executive Inn? It was Josh Kirkland."

"Oh, no!"

Chelsea released his arm to cover her mouth with her hand at the same moment Sheriff Maguire reached Mr. Kirkland.

"I've been looking all over the place for you, Les."

Derrick heard those words clearly, then the sheriff leaned over and whispered for a few seconds. The other man, eyes fixed on the sheriff's face, jerked backward in the pew.

"No. No, I don't believe it." His shout filled the sanctuary. The music stopped as the startled musicians jerked to a halt.

Sheriff Maguire nodded. "I'm sorry, Les. I've seen him. It's Josh, all right."

Mr. Kirkland stared at the sheriff, disbelief etched on his face. Then he leaped to his feet. "Momma! I've got to get to my mother. He's…" A sob choked off his voice, and he grasped the back of the pew in front of him. "He was her youngest. This is gonna kill her."

A helpless compassion seized Derrick as he watched the grief-stricken man stumble to the rear of the sanctuary. Sheriff Maguire followed. Derrick looked toward the front, at Jazzy. The pity etched on her face as she stared after the two made his throat tight.

FOUR

Jazzy stood in the parking lot beside Liz and Caitlin, watching Derrick unlock his truck. She tried not to turn up her nose at the crusty dirt that lined the rear wheel well and splattered the back fender. This was a small, country town surrounded by farmland, after all. Maybe he'd gotten stuck in the mud and hadn't had time to get to a carwash yet.

"There you go." He threw the passenger door open and held a hand out to assist Caitlin in climbing into the backseat.

Jazzy gave Liz a narrow-lidded glance and tipped her head toward the front seat while Derrick wasn't looking. Hopefully Liz understood she was calling shotgun. One side of Liz's mouth twitched upward at the wordless message, but at least she climbed without argument into the backseat beside Caitlin.

Jazzy preferred cars, but at least Derrick's truck seemed to have plenty of room. A glance inside showed her the backseat was almost as big as her Buick's. Derrick held a hand toward her to help her step up.

A warm tingling engulfed her fingers as she grasped his hand. A glance into his face showed her he felt the delicious contact, too. The intensity in his eyes deepened. Her gaze fell away and a thrill buzzed through her head and warmed her cheeks. She placed a foot on the running board—

—and stopped. A white paper bag and two crumpled napkins littered the seat she was about to climb into.

"Oh. Sorry about that." Derrick reached past her and swept his free hand across the seat, knocking the trash to the floor and then sliding it under the seat. "Sorry."

Jazzy stared with distaste at the floorboard. "But…"

"It's just an empty bag and a couple of napkins. I went to the drive-through on the way to work this morning and forgot to take my trash inside."

Forgot to take his trash… Jazzy suppressed a shudder. How people could leave litter lying around was beyond her understanding. It was such a simple matter to pick it up and put it in a proper trash receptacle. She started to volunteer to take Derrick's trash back into the church, but a glance into the backseat at her friends' faces made her stop. They were both trying to smother grins.

Setting her teeth together, Jazzy climbed into the truck. His hand lingered on hers as she settled herself in, then he shut the door. While he rounded the front of the pickup she reached beneath the seat. Before he got to the driver's side she stuffed the napkins into the bag and plucked the empty foam coffee cup out of the console cup holder, shoving that in, too.

Derrick opened the door and caught her as she slid open the ashtray and scooped out an assortment of paper, gum wrappers and bottle caps. One blond eyebrow rose in a silent question.

"I'll take it into the hotel and throw it away for you," she volunteered.

Derrick hefted himself up and slid behind the wheel. "You don't have to do that."

"Oh, yes, she does." Laughter infused Liz's tone. "Jazzy is the ultimate neatnick."

"Yeah, you know Monica on *Friends?*" Jazzy glared toward

the backseat, but that didn't shut Caitlin up. "Jazzy's apartment makes hers look like the inside of a Dumpster."

"Really?" A grin hovered around Derrick's mouth. "Then we'd better pray the hotel has found you all a room. Monica here would probably have a fit over the dishes stacked in my sink."

"Dirty dishes?" Jazzy couldn't help it. Her nose wrinkled. "You mean you just put them in there and left them?"

Derrick shifted the truck into Reverse. He placed an arm across the back of her seat and turned to look out the rear window as he backed up. "Yeah, but they're not really dirty. I let the dog lick them clean first."

He let… Jazzy's throat convulsed while Liz's and Caitlin's laughter filled the truck cab.

Derrick glanced at her as he shifted into First, laughter in his eyes. Jazzy relaxed. He was just teasing her.

"You're not a dog fan?" he asked.

Jazzy hesitated. She didn't really have anything against dogs, as long as they were kept clean. But some people who owned dogs treated them like children. Was he one of those? "I've never had a dog," she said carefully.

"Oh, you'd love Old Sue." Derrick's enthusiasm told Jazzy he was probably one of those. "She's the best bird dog in three counties. I got her when she was just a pup—bought her off a guy up near Cincinnati. She goes everywhere with me."

If his dog went everywhere with him, that meant she probably rode in this truck. If so, where did she sit? Jazzy tried not to be obvious as she examined the seat around her legs, looking for dog hair.

"So do you hunt, Derrick?" Caitlin asked.

Hunt? Jazzy threw a startled glance at Derrick as he nodded. "Sure do. Been hunting since I was a boy. Whenever I'm not fishing, that is. Old Sue goes with me on the boat, too."

Dismayed, Jazzy fixed her stare through the windshield. Derrick Rogers was probably the most handsome guy she'd ever met, and judging from the way his touch lingered on her hand when he helped her into the truck, there was no doubt the attraction was mutual. But he hunted, fished, didn't wash the dirt off his truck and didn't throw his trash away. And since he lived out here in the middle of nowhere, he probably didn't frequent the symphony, either.

Let's see. A gorgeous Christian guy with whom she had nothing in common, and a dead body in her bathtub. This trip had turned into a total disaster on every front.

"My dear ladies, please accept my sincere apologies! I am horrified—*no!* I'm beyond horrified that guests of mine have been inconvenienced in such an appalling manner."

Inconvenienced was an odd way to describe being displaced from their hotel room by a host of police officers and a murder victim. But if Jazzy had felt the slightest temptation to complain, the manager's obvious eagerness to appease her and her friends stopped the words before they could form. The teenage clerk, the same one who'd checked them in this afternoon, sat with her nose in a paperback as the man came around the desk, wringing his hands. He wore a look of such sincere regret Jazzy found herself wanting to reassure him.

Apparently Caitlin felt the same. "It wasn't your fault, Mr...."

The man stopped short and put a hand to his chest. "Forgive my manners. Bradley Goggins. I'm the manager, and on behalf of the Executive Inn I want to extend my sincere apologies." He bent slightly at the waist. Odd to find such old-world manners in the middle of a country town like Waynesboro.

"That's fine." Liz's eyelids slitted. "As long as you have another room for us, Mr. Goggins."

His hand left his chest to wave in the air. "Don't give it another thought. I've already arranged for you to have a suite overlooking the river." He lowered his voice and leaned forward, his gaze circling the lobby. "We're booked to capacity, but we always keep that suite in reserve in case Mr. Harris comes to town. But he's visiting his property in Chicago this weekend."

Derrick, leaning against the counter, must have caught Jazzy's blank look. "Harris owns this place."

Bradley nodded, eyes wide. "He will be furious when he hears of this unfortunate, uh…" his fingers drew circles in the air as he searched for a word "…accident."

The image of the body loomed in Jazzy's mind. Accident? No way. She started to protest, but Derrick beat her to it. "I'd hardly call committing a grisly murder in a bathtub and covering the body with barbecue sauce an *accident.*"

Bradley winced. "Quite so. But it's just so disturbing to think that someone was—" he gulped and lowered his voice "—*murdered* right here in my hotel."

He wrung his hands together with such intensity that Jazzy wondered if he and the victim were acquainted. Then she realized they must have been. The radio station was right here in the lobby.

"When we checked in we noticed a radio station in the corner of the lobby." She nodded toward the far corner. "Did the victim broadcast from here?"

"Oh, yes. The main station is a few miles out of town in a grimy little building." Bradley shuddered. "Mr. Kirkland preferred being in the center of activity. He convinced Mr. Harris to let him set up a satellite broadcast booth here several years ago. Mr. Kirkland could be quite charming when he wanted to."

Bradley's lips snapped shut. He whirled toward the chest-high counter and shuffled an untidy pile of festival brochures into a neat stack.

So the hotel owner liked the victim, but Bradley apparently wasn't crazy about him. Interesting. Jazzy exchanged a glance with Derrick, who shrugged an eyebrow. If Josh Kirkland worked here, that would explain why he was in the hotel. But what was he doing in one of the rooms on the fourth floor?

Before Jazzy could ask the question, Liz interrupted. "I don't know about you, but I'm tired of standing around talking. Do you mind telling us where our room is?"

Caitlin nodded in agreement.

"Of course. Emmy." Bradley snapped his fingers at the teenager behind the desk. "Where are those keys?"

Without looking up from her book, Emmy picked up a small envelope identical to the one she had given Jazzy earlier. She handed it over the counter to Bradley and turned a page.

Bradley's eyelids closed, and his face tilted toward the ceiling as though in a silent prayer for patience. Then he smiled at Jazzy and handed her the envelope. "Order whatever you like from room service. It's on the house. And I'll have someone bring your bags up immediately." He looked around the floor for their luggage.

Derrick straightened. "They're in my pickup out front." His gaze bounced from Liz to Caitlin, and came to rest on Jazzy. "But I was hoping—I mean, Chelsea was hoping you'd join us at the rehearsal dinner."

Caitlin shook her head. "Not me, thanks. I'm going to have a shower, put my pj's on and go to bed." She smiled at Bradley. "Dinner on a tray sounds perfect."

"Me, too," Liz agreed.

A sudden wave of weariness made Jazzy waver on her feet. A glance at her watch told her it was only five-thirty, not even close to her bedtime. But this had been a stress-filled day, and she was tired. Dressing up for dinner, even with the promise of spending time with the handsome brother of the bride, sounded like too much effort. Aware of Derrick's hopeful glance, she shook her head.

"Please tell your sister we appreciate the offer, but today has been rather eventful." She gave a small smile at the understatement. "I think we're all ready for it to end."

"Derrick!" a female voice called from across the lobby. They all turned to see an overweight woman bearing down on them with surprising speed, anxious creases lining her broad forehead. Her vivid yellow T-shirt proclaimed in glittery red letters, Little Princess Pageant—Who Will Wear the Crown? She ran up to Derrick and threw her arms around him.

"Kate, what's wrong?" Derrick patted her back with an awkward gesture, throwing Jazzy a helpless gaze over one round shoulder.

"Haven't you heard?" Kate drew back to look at him through round eyes. "Josh Kirkland was murdered today, right here in this hotel."

There's that image again. Jazzy suppressed a shudder.

Bradley moaned. "Do you have to say that so loud?" He glanced around the lobby.

Derrick ignored him and squeezed Kate's shoulder before releasing it. "I didn't realize you and Kirkland were close."

"Oh, we weren't. We only knew each other through the pageant." She included Jazzy, Caitlin and Liz in her glance as she spoke. "He's been a volunteer for the past five years." She cocked her head and gave them a questioning look. "I don't think I've met your friends."

"Sorry. This is Jasmine, Liz and Caitlin." Derrick gestured toward each of them in turn. "They're the ensemble Chelsea hired to play at her wedding tomorrow night. They drove down from Lexington this afternoon."

At least Derrick didn't mention Jazzy finding the body. The less she had to talk about that, the better.

The creases in Kate's forehead cleared. "Musicians! Perfect! I don't suppose any of you have pageant experience, do you?" Her eager gaze bounced from Jazzy to Liz to Caitlin. Jazzy shook her head, as did her friends. "No matter. You have performance experience, so you'll be fine."

"Fine for what?" Jazzy glanced at Derrick. What was the woman talking about?

Derrick shook his head. "I know where you're going with this. It won't work."

Bradley clapped his hands together, eyes wide. "Of course! And there are three of them."

"Exactly." Kate looked at each of them eagerly. "Which of you wants to do the pageant?"

Jazzy and Caitlin exchanged confused glances. "Do what with the pageant?"

Derrick explained, "They want one of you to be a judge. Kate is the coordinator for the Little Princess Pageant, and Kirkland's death has left her short one judge."

"Three, actually." Bradley's expressive hands gestured wildly as he explained. "Mr. Kirkland was also going to judge the barbecue, burgoo and Miss Bar-B-Q competitions. We found a replacement for the adult pageant, but the guy won't touch the others. I'm on the festival committee, and we've been scrambling for the past few hours to come up with three substitutes. What luck there are three of you, one for each contest!"

Jazzy was about to protest when Derrick beat her to it. "They have to be at the church for Chelsea's wedding tomorrow at five-thirty."

"Perfect." Kate stepped sideways, cutting Derrick out of their circle. "The pageant is at three. It'll be over in plenty of time."

Bradley drew close. "And the food judging takes place Saturday at noon. You're staying two nights, aren't you?"

Liz frowned. "We were planning to get an early start toward home Saturday morning."

He dismissed that with a wave. "What's a few hours in exchange for the opportunity to taste world-class barbecue and burgoo?"

"And you'd be doing us a huge favor," Kate added.

Bradley clasped his hands beneath his chin. "Please?"

The edges of Jazzy's resistance crumbled. What would it hurt to stay a few extra hours and help them out?

Derrick stepped around Kate, scowling. "The answer is no."

Jazzy narrowed her lids at him. That was pretty presumptuous of him, making their decisions for them.

"Come on, Derrick." Kate's tone took on a pleading note. "It's just a couple of hours. They'll be done in plenty of time for the wedding."

"And they'll have fun," Bradley added. He grinned at the three of them. "The Bar-B-Q Festival is *the* event of the year in Waynesboro. You'll be famous."

Why were they trying to convince Derrick, like he was their boss or something? Just because he hired them to play a wedding didn't give him the right to monopolize their entire weekend.

Derrick folded his arms across his chest. "I said no. They're not going to do it."

Jazzy's temper flared. *Who does this country boy think he is, answering for me as if I'm not here?* Her spine stiffened as she drew herself up to her full height. "I think it sounds like fun."

Derrick's wasn't the only shocked expression that turned her way. Liz and Caitlin stared at her as though she'd lost her mind.

"Are you kidding?" Liz asked. "You would voluntarily eat road-kill stew?"

Actually, Jazzy preferred the barbecue contest. She'd tried burgoo once. That was enough.

Caitlin spoke up. "I like burgoo. My granny used to cook up a batch every year."

Bradley beamed, but Derrick's scowl deepened. He grabbed Jazzy's arm and tried to guide her away from the circle. "This is not a good idea."

Jazzy resisted his pull and stood her ground. She looked around him to catch Liz's eye. "Have you ever judged a beauty pageant?"

"Forget it." Liz's chin rose stubbornly. "I can handle barbecue, but a stage full of kids prancing around in evening gowns? Not a chance."

Discomfort fluttered in Jazzy's stomach. She'd been solo on a stage a few times herself. The memory of those icy fingers of panic played at the edges of her mind. She gave herself a mental shake. It wouldn't be her up there this time. She'd be a spectator, that's all.

Derrick was shaking his head, his lips drawn into a disapproving line.

She raised her chin and spoke to Kate and Bradley. "We'll do it."

Kate clutched Jazzy's hand. "I can't tell you how much I appreciate this. Just come to the International Ballroom down that hall tomorrow about ten minutes till three. I'll explain everything then. I've got to get back in there and leave instructions to make sure they set up the room right." She gave a final squeeze, then practically danced toward the ballroom.

Bradley clapped his hands, eyeing Liz and Caitlin with undisguised delight. "I'll let the festival committee know." He stepped forward and put an arm around each of them. "The judges are meeting tomorrow at noon, down the street at the VFW. Meet me here in the lobby and I'll walk with you." He launched into an explanation of the tasting procedures.

Derrick put a hand under Jazzy's elbow and pulled her a few steps away, shaking his head. "This is a mistake."

Jazzy ignored the warmth that spread through her arm at his touch. Instead she focused on retaining the irritation she'd felt a moment before. Hard to do with him looking down at her through those warm brown eyes. "Don't worry. We'll be on time for the wedding."

"That's not what I'm worried about." He lowered his voice and leaned toward her. "Have you considered what you're doing?"

His breath felt warm on her cheek. Jazzy shook her head to clear the giddiness that tried to invade her brain. "What are you talking about?"

His worried glance rose from hers and circled the lobby. "By stepping in to judge those contests, you'll be taking the place of a murder victim. What if…"

He didn't finish the question. He didn't have to. Jazzy's mouth dried in an instant.

FIVE

Derrick helped Bradley unload the girls' bags from the back of his pickup. "I wish you hadn't done that." He hefted a soft-sided blue suitcase onto the luggage cart.

"Done what?" Bradley said as he dragged a duffel bag to the edge of the truck bed and muttered an "humph" as he lifted it by the handle. "They'll have fun. It'll give them a good impression of Waynesboro." He dropped it onto the cart and looked down the street toward the festival route, a sour expression on his face. "As good an impression as is possible of this one-horse town, anyway."

Derrick bit back a sharp retort. He didn't know Bradley Goggins well, but the guy had obviously been miserable here since Harris had brought him down from Chicago two years ago to manage the Executive Inn. He sure hadn't made many friends with his arrogant, big-city attitude.

"Why don't you judge the burgoo and barbecue contests?"

The man slapped a hand to his chest and thrust his nose upward. "I am a vegetarian."

"Well, you could have found somebody else, then."

The automatic doors swooshed open, and Kate came through, speaking loudly into her cell phone. She ignored them as she walked by, intent on telling whoever was on the other end that she'd found a replacement judge for tomorrow's pageant. Derrick shook his head. The entire town would know before bedtime.

Bradley set the cello case on the cart and straightened. "Who would I find to judge? Nobody wants to get involved. No matter who wins, three-fourths of the town won't speak to the judges for months because their favorite cooking team lost."

Derrick tucked Jazzy's fiddle case securely beside the duffel bag. Unfortunately, Bradley had a point. The people in this town took the festival contests seriously. No cash prizes were awarded, but a lot of prestige went along with the right to display the winner's trophy, or wear the pageant crowns.

A police cruiser pulled beneath the covered entryway as Derrick slammed the tailgate closed. It stopped with a squeak of old brakes behind two other cruisers still parked there. When the door opened, the static of a two-way radio carried to Derrick's ears, followed by a female dispatcher's voice. Sheriff Maguire slammed the door and came toward them, his swagger evident even in the three short steps it took to cross the driveway.

He nodded at Derrick. "Everything go all right at the rehearsal?"

"Sure did." Derrick jingled his key ring. "I'm heading home to get cleaned up. You going to make it out to dinner?"

"You bet I am. I'm paying for the thing, ain't I? I'll be along right after I talk to those musicians." He pushed the brim of his hat up with a pointer finger as his gaze slid to Bradley. "I'll want to talk to you, too, Goggins. How late you figure on hanging around?"

Bradley heaved an exaggerated sigh. "I've already told your deputies everything I know."

The sheriff tucked a thumb in the top of his loaded utility belt. His eyes hardened. "Yeah, and you're gonna say it again to me. Maybe even twice."

Bradley stood up under Sheriff Maguire's stare for about three seconds before his shoulders drooped. "I'm not going anywhere tonight. I'll be in my office when you're ready to talk to me."

Derrick turned his head to hide a grin. Waynesboro might be a small town, but its sheriff could hold his own with any big-city cop.

"I'll see you at the restaurant, then," Derrick said, then headed around the side of his pickup toward the cab as Bradley pushed the luggage cart toward the hotel entrance. Derrick opened the truck door and hesitated, Jazzy's exhausted face fresh in his mind. "Hey, Sheriff?" Maguire turned to look at him as the automatic doors swooshed open. "Go easy on them, okay? They've had a rough day."

The sheriff straightened his shoulders, a stubborn set coming over his jaw. "There's a killer loose in our town, Rogers. I ain't planning to go easy on anybody till we catch him." One eyebrow rose. "Or her."

Nerves tingling, Jazzy led her friends down the hallway toward their new room. Derrick was right. She should never have volunteered them to judge these contests.

Lord, what was I thinking?

She tapped the electronic key card envelope against the palm of her other hand as she walked. Thinking was exactly what she had not done. Reacting was a better description. But Derrick's attitude had been so infuriating, as though he were her father or something. She'd been determined to show him she wasn't about to be told what she could and couldn't do. Especially by some country boy who took his dog out to shoot Donald Duck on the weekends.

Except she should have at least listened to him before she jumped into the shoes of a murdered man. And dragged her friends with her.

She stopped in front of the door to room 197 and cast an anxious look at Liz. "Are you worried?"

"That there's another body on the other side of that door?"

"No, I mean about judging the barbecue contest." Jazzy lowered her voice. "The victim's body was covered in barbecue sauce, after all."

Caitlin's eyes went round. "I didn't think of that. What if his death was related to the competition?"

Liz dismissed that idea with a blast of air expelled through pursed lips. "No way. The killer was probably some local yokel who used barbecue sauce to throw the cops off the trail."

Jazzy shook her head. "I don't know, Liz. The timing, the evidence—"

Liz snatched the envelope out of Jazzy's hand. "You don't know about any evidence outside of what you saw. For all you know the victim was a drug-dealing, two-timing cheat, and his sins finally caught up with him."

The sound of high-pitched giggles echoed down the hallway, warning them of the approach of a trio of little girls. Wet hair plastered their skulls, and their swimsuit-clad bodies were wrapped in thin white towels with the Executive Inn monogram stamped on one edge. One of the girls whispered into the ear of another as they passed, and the two burst into peals of laughter.

Liz scowled after them. "If you ask me, I'd say there's a bigger chance the murder has something to do with that stupid beauty pageant than the barbecue contest. Kids can be vicious, you know." She extracted one of the cards and slid it through the slot on the door.

Caitlin followed, giving Jazzy a worried look. Jazzy stared after the kids. They looked to be around twelve. Probably three of the contestants she'd judge tomorrow. A new shudder rippled through her. She hated beauty pageants.

Liz's voice continued from inside the room. "And even if his death is related to the barbecue contest, I'm from out of town. Nobody has any reason to kill me. Wow. Would you look at this place?"

Jazzy brushed away the lingering uneasiness and followed her friends. She came to a stop inside the door. "'Wow' is right."

The room was twice the size of their previous one, and it wasn't even the bedroom. When Bradley said they would have a suite, Jazzy assumed that meant they'd get a room with a kitchenette. But this was a true suite. The great room in which she stood boasted a full kitchen to her right, a glass dining table with four chairs and a comfortable living room area. The sofa and love seat were angled to face a large-screen plasma television set. The curtains had been pulled back from a sliding glass door, and through the glass Jazzy glimpsed sunlight glittering on the rippled surface of the Kentucky River.

Caitlin peeked through an open doorway on the other side of a full-size refrigerator. "There's another TV in here. Still only two beds, though."

Liz dropped onto the sofa. "That's okay. I think this thing folds out. I don't mind sleeping here. Besides, I didn't tell you something." She gave them each a sheepish grin. "I snore. You two might want to close the door."

That settled, they began investigating their suite. Jazzy was bent over, checking out the lower kitchen cabinets, which were spotless, when a loud knock sounded on the door. She jumped upright.

Caitlin laughed. "Relax. It's probably our luggage."

Better safe than sorry with a killer on the loose, Jazzy thought as she tiptoed to the door and peeked through the peephole. Relief softened her tense muscles at the telescopic image of Bradley. She unlocked the dead bolt and swung the door open.

A uniformed police officer stood beside the hotel manager. Correction. Not a police officer. A silver pin over his left pocket proclaimed him to be Sheriff Sam Maguire.

"Miss Delaney," Bradley began, but the sheriff cut him off.

"You're the one who found the murder victim." His brusque statement was not a question, but Jazzy nodded anyway. "I want to talk to you."

He elbowed his way around Bradley and brushed past Jazzy into the room without being asked. Bradley caught her with a glance and lifted his eyes toward the ceiling. Then he gestured toward a cart piled with their luggage.

"May I come in?" he asked deliberately.

"Of course." Jazzy backed up and held the door open as he wheeled the cart past her. He ignored the sheriff and headed for the bedroom.

"I hope everything is to your liking," he called over his shoulder.

Jazzy followed him as Caitlin and Liz introduced themselves to the sheriff. "This is a terrific suite. Thank you so much for letting us use it."

Bradley hefted Caitlin's duffel bag off the cart and tossed it onto the first bed. Hiding a wince, Jazzy hurried to grab her violin case before he could treat it with similar disregard.

"I finally got in touch with Mr. Harris an hour ago. He was horrified, of course, and told me to do whatever I can to make you comfortable for your entire stay. Whatever you want is on the house." Liz's suitcase landed beside Caitlin's bag with a bounce, then Bradley extracted a small card from his breast pocket. "Just show this and you'll be taken care of anywhere in the hotel. The restaurant. The business center. There's a nice lounge in the west corner of the lobby if you'd care for a cocktail before dinner."

Jazzy took the card, but shook her head with a smile. "Thanks, but we don't drink."

"Oh." He seemed momentarily nonplussed. Then his face cleared. "They make a mean Shirley Temple down there."

She laughed. "Please tell Mr. Harris we appreciate everything."

He hefted the last suitcase onto the bed. "Call me if you need anything." His glance slid to the door. "And don't let Buford Pusser in there rattle you."

Working hard to hide her smile, Jazzy joined the others as Bradley let himself out. A glance at Sheriff Maguire's stern face chased away all remnants of the smile.

"Shall we sit down?" The sheriff pulled a padded swivel chair out from the table.

Jazzy slid into the one across from him, Liz and Caitlin taking the other two. Sheriff Maguire leaned against the seat back and folded his arms across his chest.

"Tell me what happened. All of it. From the beginning."

Irritation twitched Jazzy's frazzled nerves. She'd told this story four times to the deputies, and then had written out a statement and signed it. Did they think she was lying? Maybe they were trying to trip her up.

Any protest she might have made faded before the piercing gaze leveled across the table at her. She rubbed sweaty palms on her jeans, then stopped when the sheriff's eyes lowered to watch her hands through the glass tabletop.

For the fifth time that day, Jazzy recounted how Derrick had sent an e-mail three months ago saying he'd seen in her online profile that she played violin in a classical ensemble. She described their brief e-mail discussion establishing the terms of the job for his sister's wedding. As she did, she realized that Sheriff Maguire probably knew all about that part, since his son was the groom. Then she outlined every detail she could remember from the time they pulled up to the front doors of the Executive Inn until she opened the shower curtain.

At least Sheriff Maguire listened without interrupting. Those two deputies hadn't let her get a sentence out without a question or two. When she finished, he sat watching her in silence, tapping his pursed lips with an index finger. Jazzy shifted her position on the cushioned seat. The man's stare put her in mind of spotlights and rubber hoses.

Caitlin cleared her throat, drawing his attention away from Jazzy. "Do you have any idea why someone might have killed that poor man?"

Liz interrupted before he could answer. "What she really wants to know is if you think we're in any danger since we're taking his place as judges in this festival thing."

One of the sheriff's eyebrows rose as he shifted his gaze to Liz. "I hadn't heard that."

"It happened just after we came back from the rehearsal," Jazzy told him. "The hotel manager said they needed three judges, and since there are three of us, it seemed like a good solution."

She tried to filter the anxiety out of her voice, but in the past twenty minutes she'd begun to wonder if there was a way to get out of their commitment. She glanced at Liz, the new barbecue judge. Why hadn't she kept her mouth shut down in the lobby? If anything happened to either of her friends, Jazzy wouldn't be able to live with herself.

Liz caught the glance and rolled her eyes. "I told her there was nothing to worry about. It probably wasn't even related to the barbecue contest."

"Oh, I think it is." The sheriff moved his finger-tapping to the arm of the chair. "This festival holds a lot of weight around these parts. The team that takes top honors in the barbecue competition wins bragging rights for a whole year, and they sure exercise them. Same with the burgoo contest. But I can't see why you'd be in any danger. I'm betting this is a local job. Wouldn't surprise me if somebody tried to buy Kirkland's vote and things turned bad. We're questioning the other judges to see if any of them have had any offers."

Jazzy shook her head. "But why would Mr. Kirkland be in a room up on the fourth floor? His radio station is down in the lobby."

Sheriff Maguire shrugged. "We don't know that he was. Maybe the body was moved there."

Jazzy's teeth clamped together. That didn't make sense. Why would someone carry a grown man's body up to the fourth floor? It was too risky—they could have been spotted.

"Have you questioned the hotel staff? Maybe someone saw something suspicious. Housekeeping, for instance. When was the last time they cleaned that room?" She tilted her forehead toward him. "The sheets on that bed smelled a little stale."

"Now see here, missy." Jazzy bristled at the condescending title, but the sheriff didn't seem to notice. His fingers clutched the edge of the glass table as he pushed himself back. "You leave the investigating to us. We know what we're doing." He got to his feet and leaned forward on his hands, glancing toward Liz. "You girls are gonna be just fine. I've got two men stationed up on the fourth floor outside that room, making sure nobody touches anything before the lab boys from over at state police headquarters get here. That'll be hours yet. My deputies ain't going nowhere before sunup. Nobody's gonna mess with you with two deputies right here in the hotel."

Jazzy cast a quick glance toward Liz before she said, "Maybe we should have one outside our door, too."

Liz heaved a sigh. "That's really not necessary," she told the sheriff.

He came around the table and gave a paternal pat to Jazzy's shoulder. "If it'll make you feel better, I'll tell my boys to keep an ear open in this direction."

If there was anything worse than being afraid, it was being patronized. Jazzy gritted her teeth and rose to follow him to the door. He stepped through and then turned to face her.

"You be sure and let me know if somebody wants to talk to you about that barbecue contest, hear?"

An uneasy lump rose up to clog Jazzy's throat. Wordlessly, she nodded. She closed the door behind him and turned the dead bolt with a vicious twist.

SIX

The rehearsal dinner was well underway when Derrick finally saw Sheriff Maguire slip into the room and edge his way toward the head table. Derrick noticed the disapproving set to Mrs. Maguire's jaw as her husband slid into the empty chair beside her. At least the guy had found the time to exchange his uniform for a suit. That ought to gain him a few points with the missus.

"Sorry I'm late." The sheriff nodded at his son and Chelsea. "Got tied up over at the hotel questioning the witnesses."

"It's okay, Dad. We understand." Quinn poked him with an elbow and grinned. "To make it up to us, we'll let you give a toast to your new daughter-in-law at the reception tomorrow."

"That will be my pleasure."

Beside Derrick, Mom set down her iced-tea and leaned toward him. Worry deepened the creases between her hazel eyes as she spoke in a whisper. "It's just terrible what happened to that Kirkland boy. His mother must be devastated."

Ever since Dad had passed away, Mom felt death keenly, even when it happened to someone she didn't know.

Derrick covered her hand with his. "Don't think about it. Tonight is all about the bride and the groom." He squeezed her hand and smiled. "And the beautiful mother of the bride."

A blush identical to her daughter's colored her cheeks, and

she pulled her hand away. "Oh, you!" But she dimpled as she smiled, and Derrick was glad he'd managed to get her mind off of her dark thoughts.

As Mom turned away to say something to Chelsea, Derrick glanced at his watch. It had been almost two hours since he'd left the Executive Inn. Hopefully Jazzy and her friends were settling in for a peaceful night.

Caitlin shuffled from the bathroom past Jazzy's bed in fuzzy slippers. "Will it bother you if I turn on the television? I could go out and watch the big one with Liz for a while if you want to go to sleep now."

Propped against the headboard on two pillows, Jazzy flipped through the latest issue of *Music & Vision*. She shook her head. "Won't bother me. I have a timer on my stereo at home so I can fall asleep to music."

Of course, the soothing strains of Pachelbel were far more conducive to sleep than barking dogs on *Animal Cops*. Jazzy didn't say anything, though. Friendships were all about being tolerant of one another, especially when traveling.

She closed her magazine and turned off the lamp mounted on the wall between the two beds. The sheets smelled good as she slid between them, like her favorite brand of fabric softener. She rolled onto her side, away from the flickering lights of the television screen. The delicious dinner delivered by room service sat comfortably in her tummy. A tide of drowsiness washed across the shores of her mind. She closed her eyes and let her worries drift out of reach. The sheriff wasn't worried. Liz wasn't worried. Why should she be? She welcomed slumber as it crept gently over her.

Sometime later, a sound intruded on her dream. Or was it part of her dream? Jazzy couldn't tell, but the foggy tendrils of sleep fell slowly away and she became aware of her surroundings.

The comforting weight of the bedspread. The soft cotton sheets. The quiet snuffle of Caitlin's breathing in the next bed. The distant sound of the television set from the other room. She didn't remember when Caitlin had turned off the TV in their room, but Liz had apparently fallen asleep with hers on. Jazzy vaguely remembered hearing her snoring earlier, the sound muted through the closed door.

Liz wasn't snoring at the moment. Maybe that's what had awakened Jazzy. Not a sound, but the cessation of a sound to which she'd grown accustomed. She lay there, slumber flirting with her thoughts, lulling them back into the dream she'd left too early. A few moments passed, and Liz's snore started again. Her eyes closed, Jazzy extended an arm from the shelter of the blanket and fumbled for the extra pillow. She laid it across her head as a sound buffer for her ear, then relaxed even more deeply into the mattress. *Now, what was that dream...*

A scream pierced the night. Jazzy jerked upright. Beside her, Caitlin scrambled out of bed and raced toward the door. Jazzy leaped from beneath the blanket, one step behind her. They dashed through the doorway.

Something moved on the patio. She saw a dark silhouette against the moonlight shining on the river. An instant later it was gone. The sliding glass door stood open. A cold breeze laden with the scent of the river invaded the room.

Jazzy flipped the wall switch. Liz sat in the center of her bed, gasping, her hands clutching her throat. Panic filled her wide eyes.

"He tried to strangle me!"

A crazy numbness seemed to have attacked Jazzy's feet. They refused to move. Horror crept up her spine on prickly legs.

Caitlin ran to the bed and threw her arms around Liz. "Are you all right? Are you hurt?" She twisted her head to look at Jazzy without letting go of Liz. "Call 9-1-1," she ordered.

Nodding, Jazzy stepped toward the desk. Hand trembling, she reached for the receiver. One part of her brain registered the fact that papers lay strewn across the surface of the desk. Sheet music, and the advertisement brochures they'd put together about their trio. The intruder must have dumped the contents of their music portfolios. They'd set them on the desk in readiness for the wedding tomorrow.

Then her gaze fell on something else resting on the desk. Something that had not been there before.

A bottle of barbecue sauce.

Invisible steel bands tightened around Jazzy's chest.

SEVEN

Jazzy and Caitlin huddled in a corner, hands clasped for comfort. Jazzy watched as a female EMT examined Liz's neck. The woman's male partner stood at the foot of the sofa bed, and a uniformed deputy watched the proceedings from a position near the door.

"I'm fine, really. I don't need to go to the hospital." The surly cellist pushed the woman's hands away and leaned against the back cushion of the fold-out couch. "He scared me more than anything."

The deputy standing nearby perked up. "He? You're sure it was a man who attacked you?"

"Well…" Liz screwed up her face, thinking. "I *think* it was a man. I mean, I can't be positive. The room was dark and he wore some sort of mask. I woke to find him looming over me." Her hands hovered around her throat in an unconscious gesture, a haunted expression darkening her features. "He had really strong hands."

Guilt rose up in Jazzy's throat like bile. She squeezed Caitlin's fingers. This was her fault. If she hadn't been trying to prove to Derrick that she couldn't be bossed around, Liz wouldn't have been attacked.

An authoritative knock sounded on the door. When the deputy opened it, Jazzy wasn't surprised to see Sheriff Maguire stride into the room. Instead of the crisp uniform he had worn earlier, he'd thrown on a pair of gray trousers and a dark T-shirt with a yellow sheriff's star emblazoned on the breast pocket.

He stopped in the center of the room and let his gaze circle the occupants. It came to rest on the deputy. "What's the situation here?"

Anger flared in Jazzy, fueled by regret for her own mistake. Her guilt needed an outlet or she feared she might collapse under the weight. A likely target had just made himself available.

She dropped Caitlin's hand and took a step forward. "I'll tell you the 'situation.' You said we were safe, that we didn't need a guard. And look what happened!"

The sheriff turned a calm look her way. She stood rigid, fists clenching and unclenching, waiting for him to say something.

Instead, he turned back to the deputy. "You were saying?"

Jazzy felt Caitlin's hand on her arm. But the gentle touch failed to soothe her anger.

With a nervous gulp and a quick glance in her direction, the deputy answered his boss's question. "An intruder gained access through the patio door. Popped the lock, probably with a crowbar. The metal's bent. Slipped into the room real quiet-like, right past Miss Carmichael asleep there." He dipped his forehead toward the sofa bed. "Went through that suitcase and dumped that purse out. Shuffled through some papers. Left that." He nodded toward the bottle of sauce on the desk.

Jazzy kept her jaws locked while the sheriff walked around the room, his hands clasped behind his back. He inspected the disarray on the desk without touching anything, noted the chaos in Liz's suitcase and the contents of her purse sprawled across the love-seat cushion then peeked through the open back door.

"We got the place cordoned off?"

The deputy nodded. "Matt and Bob are taping the back of this wing off right now. The investigators from Frankfort are still processing the room upstairs, but they called for reinforcements."

Sheriff Maguire threw a long-suffering glance toward the ceiling. "Just what we need. State boys swarming all over the place on festival weekend." He glared at the deputy. "Get Frank and Kenneth in here, too. I want every man we've got working this case."

The deputy nodded and headed toward the door. Jazzy ground her teeth as the sheriff continued to ignore her. He turned his attention to the female EMT who had been examining Liz.

"She gonna be all right?"

The woman glanced at Liz and nodded. "She'll have a couple of bruises on her neck, but the intruder ran off without inflicting any real injury." She gathered up her instruments, shoved them in a bag and rose from the bed. "If you start feeling anything unusual, you call us back," she told Liz.

When the EMTs were gone, Sheriff Maguire folded an arm across his stomach, propped his other elbow on it and tapped his lips with a forefinger. He studied Liz through narrowed eyelids. "Now why do you suppose the killer ran off without finishing the job this time?"

Jazzy couldn't stop a shudder at the thought of Liz in the same shape as that man in the upstairs bathtub.

Liz lifted her shoulders. "I started kicking like crazy, and I think I landed a couple of good ones because his grip on my throat let up. That's when I screamed. Maybe I scared him away."

"So you woke up with his hands around your neck?"

Confusion creased Liz's forehead. "I—I think so." She shook her head. "No, wait a minute. Something else woke me up. A sound or something. I think now it must have been my car keys when he dumped my purse, but at the time I thought it was on television. I didn't open my eyes, just reached for the remote control where I'd left it on the coffee table. The next thing I knew…" She swallowed with an effort.

"I heard something, too." Jazzy held her gaze steady as the sheriff turned his attention to her. "Not keys jingling, more like a crack."

"The lock being popped?" Maguire asked.

Jazzy closed her eyes, trying to remember the sound. "That might have been it. I thought it was the television, too."

She turned an apologetic smile on her friend. Liz looked so vulnerable, Jazzy fought against a sudden rush of tears. She dropped onto the mattress and threw her arms around her friend's shoulders.

"I'm so sorry, Liz," she sobbed. "If I hadn't forced you to judge that contest none of this would have happened."

"It's not your fault," Liz said, returning her embrace. "You didn't force me into anything. I could have said no."

Caitlin slid onto the fold-out couch beside them. "Thank the Lord you're okay."

"Yes." Jazzy rested her forehead on Liz's shoulder and whispered, "Thank you, Lord, for keeping our friend safe." Then she raised her head and sniffed. "One thing's for sure. You're not going anywhere near that barbecue contest. They can find themselves another judge."

Sheriff Maguire's voice reminded them of his presence. "I'm not sure the barbecue contest is the cause here."

Jazzy threw him a startled look. "Of course it is. Why else would he have left *that?*" She grimaced toward the bottle on the desk.

"To throw us off. I'm beginning to think this killer is using the barbecue contest as a red herring. Especially now."

Caitlin straightened. "Why especially now?"

"Because he went through your belongings."

Jazzy looked at the mess of clothes in Liz's suitcase, the litter of music on the desk. Her music portfolio, a black leather bag with a zipper, lay discarded and empty alongside Liz's and Caitlin's. "And he dumped all our music out, too. Why would he do that?"

"He was looking for something?" Caitlin suggested.

Liz shook her head. "What could he be looking for in my suitcase or our music?"

"That's what we need to find out." Sheriff Maguire pulled a chair from beneath the table and turned it around. He perched on it backward, his arms folded across the low back. "What do you girls have that a killer would want bad enough to risk coming back to the scene of his crime for?"

Jazzy exchanged a blank look with her friends.

"Money?" Caitlin suggested. "I have a couple hundred dollars in my purse."

"Nobody could possibly know that. Hey!" Liz scrambled onto her knees and crawled toward the love seat. "I haven't checked to see if anything's missing."

Sheriff Maguire raised a hand in caution. "Look, but don't touch. We need to get some pictures and check for prints."

While Liz hovered over her suitcase and purse, Jazzy inspected the papers spread across the desk. Everything was there. All her sheet music, the brochures, a couple of pencils she kept in the portfolio for notations during rehearsal.

"I can't really tell without going through it," Liz said, "but I don't think anything's gone."

"Here, either," Jazzy agreed. "I don't get it."

"Think," the sheriff urged. "There's got to be something."

Jazzy crossed to the love seat and stood beside Liz. "What did you pack in your suitcase?"

"Clothes. Shoes. Toiletries. Nothing worth stealing."

"What about your purse?" Caitlin asked.

Liz shrugged. "The usual. A comb, a compact, lipstick. My

wallet has a little cash and a few credit cards and some family pictures and—"

"Pictures!" Jazzy jerked backward and slapped a hand on the top of her head. She whirled to Caitlin. "You were taking pictures in the lobby yesterday."

"Yeah, so?"

Sheriff Maguire straightened in the chair. "A camera. Of course."

Caitlin's eyes went round as she stared at the officer. "Do you think I got a picture of the killer?"

"You might have."

Blood roared in Jazzy's ears at the idea of the killer leaving the scene of his violent crime and calmly walking past them in the check-in line. Had he watched them, stared at them? She scrunched up her face, trying to remember. She'd told the police about the repairman and the room-service waiter. Neither of them had seemed to pay any attention to the trio of musicians at all. The only other people she could remember were the guests checking in, and the kids. Tons of kids.

Sheriff Maguire stood and pushed the chair back into position at the table. "I'll need that camera."

As Caitlin went into the bedroom to retrieve the camera, a cold night breeze blew through the open patio door. Jazzy rubbed her hands on her bare arms. Her shudder was not entirely from the chilly wind.

EIGHT

While Sheriff Maguire and his men snapped pictures and dusted for fingerprints, the girls took refuge on the other side of the bedroom door. They huddled together on Caitlin's bed, propped up on pillows with Liz in the middle. Jazzy was unwilling to separate herself from the comforting presence of her friends, even as far as her own bed. The other two apparently didn't mind. Nobody suggested she move.

"We should probably try to get some sleep," Caitlin said.

A low drone of voices filtered through the wall as the investigators talked with one another. Sheriff Maguire's baritone punctuated the buzz, his tone authoritative but the words indistinguishable.

"I don't think I can sleep with that going on." Jazzy nodded toward the door. "I wonder how long they'll be here."

"I don't know, but I feel better having them out there, don't you?" Liz shuddered.

Jazzy glanced at the clock. Glowing red numbers told her the time was after three. "I think I saw a sign that said the restaurant opens at six. We'll be able to get some coffee then." She'd noticed a coffeepot in the kitchen of their suite, but no coffee in the cabinets.

"I hope it's strong." Caitlin yawned, and both Jazzy and Liz echoed the gesture.

"We might as well try to rest." Liz scooted down in the bed and pulled her pillow into place beneath her head. "We're going to have a long day before that wedding."

"If you all don't want to stay, we could cancel the wedding gig." Caitlin glanced from Liz to Jazzy. "Pack up and go home as soon as the cops are finished with Liz's suitcase."

Jazzy tensed. Where would Chelsea find substitute musicians a few hours before her wedding? And what would Derrick think of them if they bailed out now, leaving him without an ensemble and with a possibly weepy sister on her wedding day?

On the other hand, if Liz didn't want to stay after the trauma she'd experienced, Jazzy couldn't fault her. But she couldn't ditch a bride at the last minute. She'd play solo if she had to, and rent a car to drive back home tomorrow night after the ceremony.

"You guys do whatever you think is best," she said carefully, "but I don't feel right about canceling."

"Yeah, I'm with Jazzy." Liz pulled the blanket up to her chin. "We agreed to do this gig, and we're going to do it. You know what the Bible says. God didn't give us a spirit of fear."

Jazzy was glad to hear a touch of the familiar, brash attitude in Liz's voice. She'd had a shock, but she was bouncing back.

Caitlin shrugged, then slid beneath the blanket, too. Jazzy twisted the light switch off and settled along the edge of the mattress. Slivers of light from the spotlights the police had set up outside glowed around the edges of the curtains that covered the window. She closed her eyes. Maybe her body would benefit from a few hours of quiet rest, but no way would her busy mind let her sleep. Dozens of thoughts skittered through her brain like fireflies soaring skyward from the ground at twilight.

"I can't sleep," came Caitlin's voice from the other side of the bed. "If we're going to stay for the wedding, I feel guilty about backing out of that burgoo contest."

"Guilty?" Liz assumed a professional tone. "Remember what else that verse says. We don't have a spirit of fear, but we are supposed to have a spirit of sound mind. So don't talk crazy."

But Jazzy knew what Caitlin meant. She'd been thinking the same thing, and picturing Kate's panic when she found out she was short one judge the day of the pageant. "Who else are they going to find this late? They called off their search last night when we agreed to step in. And besides, Sheriff Maguire doesn't think the murder or the attack are really related to the contest anyway."

"Are you two saying you want to stay in this hotel another night?" Liz said with disbelief.

Jazzy voiced the worry that had been nagging at the back of her mind. "What if we go home and the guy follows us?"

Silence stole over the room as Liz and Caitlin considered Jazzy's words. If the murderer was intent on getting the camera he thought they had, Jazzy would rather not lead him back to their apartments, where they would encounter him alone. Better to wait until it became public knowledge that the camera had been turned over to the police. Then they'd be safe.

"If we're going to stay another night, I'd feel safer with someone watching the doors," Caitlin said. "The sheriff might be more inclined to give us a guard now."

"We would *make* him," Jazzy insisted. "And if he doesn't," she added in a voice as matter-of-fact as she could make it, "I'll bet Derrick would stay with us."

The bed gave a violent heave. Jazzy turned her head to find both of her friends sitting up. In the dim light shining around the edges of the curtain she could just make out knowing grins on both of their faces.

"He could sleep out there on the sofa." She turned her back on them and closed her eyes.

"He is pretty cute, isn't he? No wedding ring. And he didn't mention a girlfriend, either."

Jazzy heard the smile in Liz's voice. Apparently she was ready to move beyond the chilling thoughts of the danger that surrounded them in order to prod information out of Jazzy about the handsome brother of the bride. Liz was forever trying to fix Jazzy up with some guy or other, usually friends of her own boyfriend. Jazzy detested blind dates and had consistently refused. She ignored her friend and kept her eyes shut.

"And it's obvious he likes you, Jazzy." Laughter bubbled in Caitlin's words.

A smile tried to twitch one edge of Jazzy's mouth, but she wrestled it down. "He is totally not my type. Did you see the mud on his truck? And the litter inside? Plus, he has a dog."

"Come on, Jazzy. Don't be difficult. His truck was cleaner than my car. And what's wrong with dogs?"

Jazzy refused to rise to dog-lover Caitlin's bait. "Besides, he hunts and fishes." She shuddered at the thought of Derrick handling a cold, slimy fish with his bare hands, then wanting to touch her with those same hands. It was positively nauseating.

"Glenn fishes." Caitlin's voice went soft at the mention of her boyfriend. "He might smell a little fishy when he first gets out of the boat, but it washes off."

Jazzy remained silent. Her friends settled back down into the bed.

"No matter what you say," Liz said, "I think you like him."

"You're wrong." Jazzy closed her eyes. "He's probably a nice guy—all those country-boy habits aside—but he's not my type at all."

Her friends fell silent. Eventually Caitlin's breath slowed, and Liz started to snore softly. Jazzy forced herself to release the tension that knotted her muscles, but sleep lay just beyond her grasp.

She occupied her mind by listing all the reasons a relationship with Derrick Rogers was *not* a good idea.

NINE

Jazzy watched the digital numbers on the clock change from five forty-three to five forty-four. She held her body still so as not to disturb her friends. Why hadn't she moved to the other bed so she could toss and turn at will? At least Caitlin and Liz were getting some sleep. Though how they could sleep through the voices of the police officers just outside the door, she couldn't imagine.

At five forty-five, she slipped out of bed as gently as she could. Liz's snore quieted for the span of three breaths, but then started up again. Without a sound, Jazzy grabbed some clothes from her suitcase and crept into the bathroom.

A few minutes later, dressed in jeans, a T-shirt and tennis shoes with no socks, Jazzy wedged herself through a crack in the bedroom door.

Most of the officers who had crowded the room a few hours ago were gone. A lone deputy dozed in a chair at the dinette table. Jazzy recognized him as one of the two who had questioned her yesterday, the nicer one who seemed to know Derrick. What was his name? Matt something-or-other. A rush of gratitude toward Sheriff Maguire flooded her. He'd left someone to guard them.

At the almost soundless click of the door Jazzy pulled closed behind her, Matt jerked upright and leaped to his feet. "Oh, it's you." He dug at his eyes with a thumb and forefinger. "Sorry. I must have dozed off for a minute." His shoulders straightened, eyes going wide. "But you were safe, ma'am. I promise. Nothing could have gotten by me."

The speed of his awakening at the slight sound she'd made with the door bore testimony to his words.

Jazzy kept her voice low so she wouldn't disturb her friends in the other room. "I was going to head down to the restaurant for some coffee. Would you like me to bring you some?"

"That'd be great." He started to pull his wallet out of his back pocket, but she whipped out the card Bradley had given her. "Don't worry about it. This one's on the house."

She turned toward the front door, then paused as an ugly thought occurred to her. She turned back to Matt.

"Do you think it's safe?"

A grin stole over his mouth. "Don't worry about that, ma'am."

He walked by her to the front door, threw open the dead bolt and opened it. He stuck his head into the hallway and said in a loud stage whisper, "Hey, Frank. C'mere a minute."

Jazzy followed him to the door just as another deputy arrived. Frank, the persistent one from yesterday.

Matt grinned down at her. "The sheriff's taking no chances this time. Frank here's been stationed at the end of the hall by that exit door, and we got another guy out on the back porch."

Relief settled deep in Jazzy's tense shoulders. Maybe the fit she threw at Sheriff Maguire had done some good after all.

On the other hand, if he thought they needed so many guards…

She gulped.

"She's going to the restaurant for coffee. You want to walk her there? I can handle things here for a few minutes."

Frank's jaw tightened as he bit back a yawn. He nodded. "I could use some coffee myself."

Jazzy headed for the lobby, her bodyguard in tow. She felt a little strange to have the man who questioned her so closely yesterday tagging along behind her today. But at least his presence gave her a sense of security. Nobody would bother her with an armed guard close on her heels.

The lobby wasn't nearly as active as the day before, but a small amount of comforting activity was in evidence in several places. The quiet hum of a vacuum cleaner operated by a hotel housekeeper drifted across the expanse of the lobby toward Jazzy. Another maid rubbed a polishing rag around the edges of the elevators. Behind the front desk, the head of a young man was just visible as he sat in the chair of the girl who had checked Jazzy and her friends in yesterday.

Letters announcing the location of the Executive Café blazed in red neon over the entrance to the restaurant. Jazzy stepped through, the deputy right behind her. Apparently they were the first guests of the morning. The brown-topped tables were all empty, but two apron-clad servers stood chatting near a drink station at the opposite end of the restaurant. A third caught a glimpse of them and approached the hostess stand.

"Will that be two for breakfast?" As she spoke, she picked up two plastic-coated menus.

"No, we're just here for coffee." Jazzy smiled at the woman. "Is it ready yet?"

"Just finished brewing." She returned the menus to the stack. "Will that be to go?"

Jazzy glanced at Frank. Liz and Caitlin weren't up yet, but if Matt needed a cup of coffee, the other two deputies would probably appreciate one, too. "Four large ones."

The woman scurried off toward the back of the restaurant. Minutes later she returned with four tall cardboard coffee cups on a tray along with a handful of condiments and wooden stir sticks. The strong odor of coffee tantalized Jazzy's nose as she approached.

"We're out of lids. Sorry."

She set the tray on the checkout counter and stepped around to the cash register.

"Oh, here." Jazzy held out Bradley's complimentary card. While the woman examined it, Jazzy pulled a dollar tip out of her other pocket and handed it over. "Thanks so much."

She picked up the tray and stepped through the exit into the lobby. Frank followed, his eyes darting this way and that. Honestly, it was creepy the way he hovered behind her without speaking. If he put on some dark sunglasses he'd look sort of like Nicolas Cage in *Guarding Tess*. Maybe Frank was rehearsing for his next career, a job with the secret service.

Jazzy started to head toward their suite, but just then Bradley came through a door behind the front desk. He wore no tie, and even across the lobby Jazzy could see that he looked frazzled.

She wanted to talk to him, find out what he knew about the break-in last night. But if he knew anything, he wasn't likely to talk freely in front of her bodyguard.

Jazzy thrust the coffee-laden tray toward Frank. "Deputy, would you mind taking this back to your partners? I want to talk to the manager for a minute."

A frown creased his face, but Jazzy countered it with a confident smile. "I'm going right over there to the front desk. Then I'm coming straight back to the room. I won't leave the lobby—I promise. And when I turn that corner toward our room, you'll be able to see me from your position at the other end of the hall. I'll be fine."

She cut off any argument he might have made by shoving the tray toward his chest. His hands came up automatically. She grabbed one of the cups and held it up in a silent toast as she backed away.

Bradley caught sight of her as she crossed the lobby. He

rushed through the half door at the end of the front desk and raced toward her, hands extended.

"Oh, Miss Delaney, I can't *tell* you how sorry I am. No, how *horrified* I am." For a moment Jazzy thought he might grab her for a hug. Instead he seized her free hand and squeezed. "Are you and the other ladies all right?"

"We're fine," Jazzy assured him. "Liz was a little shook up, as you can imagine."

"No, I can't even begin to imagine the terror that poor girl must have felt. Just think. Waking up to find someone's hands at your throat." He clutched his own throat with both hands and swallowed noisily.

A thread of suspicion wove its way through Jazzy. How did he know the details of what had happened? She brought her coffee cup to her lips to hide her expression behind the steam rising from the hot liquid. Would the police have told him specifics of the attack?

"So I guess the sheriff told you all about it," she said in a casual tone.

He gave an expansive shudder. "They made the night clerk call me to come in a little after three. When I got here they grilled me for over two hours. Just left about thirty minutes ago with all the security recordings from the past month." He glanced around the lobby and lowered his voice. "What was left of them."

Okay, so details of the attack may have come out naturally as the sheriff questioned Bradley. Jazzy relaxed a fraction, then the implication of his words sank in. "Were some of the recordings missing?"

Misery suffused his face as he nodded. "Friday and Saturday from last week. We have the recording from each day on a disk, and we store them in the manager's office. I've been trying to convince Mr. Harris that we need to upgrade our equipment, but this hotel is barely paying for itself as it is." The glance that circled the lobby held a touch of bitterness. "Why should he sink money into this place when he has much nicer and more profitable hotels in big cities like Chicago?"

Jazzy sipped at the strong coffee. Two days' worth of security tapes missing. "Who has access to your office?"

"A handful of hotel employees." Bradley's chin came up. "All of them trustworthy. There's a key in a drawer behind the front desk, in case someone needs to get in there in my absence. I keep another key on my personal key ring." His shoulders sagged. "I can't imagine what Mr. Harris is going to say about this."

An idea occurred to Jazzy. Bradley said Friday and Saturday were missing. She drew an excited breath. "What about last night's recordings? Maybe you recorded the guy breaking through the patio door in our suite."

Bradley shook his head. "We don't have any external cameras. Or any internal cameras, either, except that one." He nodded toward a camera suspended from the ceiling above the front desk. "It records activity at the check-in desk, and the range goes a little beyond the counter into the lobby." He grimaced. "I told you we needed new equipment."

Jazzy's excitement deflated. "I guess the intruder didn't walk in front of the camera before he came around back and broke in."

Bradley shook his head. "I'm sure he didn't. The night clerk said it was quiet all night." One side of his lips twitched upward. "The good news is that yesterday's disk was still there. The police are going to compare it to the pictures you ladies took and see if they can identify anyone suspicious who shows up in both."

The elevator doors opened and a few early risers made their way toward the restaurant. Jazzy noticed a couple descending the stairs and a woman hovering in front of the festival event marquee. The guests of the Executive Inn were beginning to stir.

Through the glass front doors, she saw that the sky above the buildings across the street had begun to lighten, revealing a few early-morning clouds. She had forgotten to grab her watch, but it must be after six-thirty. Liz and Caitlin might be awake by now. She'd better get another couple of coffees.

She smiled at Bradley. "I'm sure you have a lot going on, so I'll let you get back to work."

"You can't imagine. The first official day of the festival." He rolled his eyes with an exaggerated gesture. "This place will be crazy for the next three days." His brow creased. "I don't suppose Miss Carmichael is feeling up to judging the barbecue competition." He placed a hand on her arm and rushed on. "Not that anyone would blame her, of course. I just need to know so I can try to scare up a replacement before the meeting at noon."

"Actually, we talked about that last night. We're prepared to honor our commitments, provided Sheriff Maguire can guarantee our safety for another night here."

Bradley winced, then acknowledged the validity of her concern with a nod. "I understand. I just wish I could move you to another room. But we're completely full, except for the one…" His head jerked toward the back wing where their first room was located.

Jazzy shuddered. "That's all right. We're hoping when word gets out that Sheriff Maguire has our camera, the killer will realize we don't know anything and he'll leave us alone. Until then, as long as that outside door can be secured and Sheriff Maguire will give us a guard, we'll be safe."

He grasped her free hand. "I'm *beyond* grateful, Miss Delaney. You and your friends are true lifesavers."

Bradley returned to the front desk, and Jazzy headed for the restaurant. Lifesavers, he called them. Well, Jazzy prayed that was true. Beginning with their own.

TEN

As Jazzy neared the restaurant entrance, someone rushed toward her.

"Miss Delaney!"

A tall woman with broad shoulders planted herself in Jazzy's path. Surprised to hear her name from a stranger, Jazzy looked up into the broad face that towered over hers. Her heart plummeted: it was the woman who had pitched a fit over her room at check-in yesterday.

"Did I hear that man call you Miss Delaney?"

The intensity in the eyes that bored into hers made Jazzy want to deny it. Had the woman been eavesdropping on her conversation with Bradley? How long had she been standing near that marquee before Jazzy noticed her? The cardboard cup in Jazzy's hand threatened to collapse as her grip tightened. She gave a cautious nod.

"Then you're the new judge for the Little Princess Pageant this afternoon."

It was a statement not requiring an answer. Nor did the woman give her time for one. Jazzy found her hand caught in the confines of a fist twice the size of her own.

"I'm Irene Baldwin. My girl Heidi is the next Little Princess."

She did not shake Jazzy's hand, but clenched it in a grip as unbreakable as the gaze that imprisoned Jazzy's eyes.

"Uh, well, I—" Jazzy stammered.

Irene cut her off. "Heidi's twelve, so this is her last year before Miss Bar-B-Q Teen." Her voice held more gravel than a country road. "Ain't nobody worked harder for it than my girl. Twirls that baton so fast you can't hardly see nothing but a flash of silver." She pronounced it *bat*-on. "She can do fire, too, 'cept'n' they won't let her here."

Jazzy was accustomed to looking up at people, but Irene towered an intimidating head and a half over her. "I look forward to seeing her perform." She tugged at her hand, hoping the woman would take the hint and let go.

Instead, the grip tightened. Jazzy winced as her college class ring cut into her finger.

"I nearly whooped when I heard we was getting a out-of-town judge. 'Bout time they seen what's been going on. Crooked, that's what they were last year. And the year before. That guy who done gone and got himself kilt was the worst."

"Mr. Kirkland?"

Irene's eyelids narrowed. "His vote was for sale, everybody knowed it. But me and Ralph, we're just plain old farm folk. We don't have a lot."

Jazzy finally managed to extract her hand. Her thumb rubbed the indentation the ring had made. "I don't understand why someone would want the Little Princess title badly enough to buy a vote. Is there a big cash prize that goes with the crown?"

Judging by Irene's clean but worn jeans and shirt, a cash award would come in handy in the Baldwin household.

"Nah, nothing like that." She lowered her voice and glanced around the lobby. "This here's a small town, but we got some folks who think they're big stuff. They don't allow no room for someone else to step into their spotlight, even for a minute."

"So it's a matter of pride."

A smirk twisted Irene's lips. "And you know what they say about pride going before a fall. I guess that Josh Kirkland fell pretty hard, didn't he?"

An icy shiver dropped Jazzy's core a couple of degrees. She couldn't imagine speaking with such venom about a murder victim. Even if she didn't like him.

"Some of them girls been given everything they wanted from the time they first drew breath. They wear fancy clothes and take their dancing lessons and all. One day they'll drive shiny cars and go off to big colleges." Irene stared at a point beyond Jazzy's head, envy glinting in her eyes. Then she doused it and looked down. "My girl Heidi, she's pretty and smart, and she's got as much talent as all of them others put together. But we don't have no money for college. She needs a break. If she wins—" Her jaw firmed. "*When* she wins, we're going up to Louisville and sign her up with a modeling agency. Too much money, Ralph says, but they told me they'll take their cut out of her earnings when she gets commercials and the like. But only if she's got a good résumé." She pronounced the word as though it were in a foreign language.

The importance of a pageant win for this woman's daughter became clear to Jazzy. "And if Heidi can put the title of Little Princess on her résumé, she'll have a better chance of signing with that agency."

Irene nodded. "My girl deserves a better life than slaving away sunup to sundown on some old farm. And I aim to see she gets it."

She caught Jazzy in an unflinching gaze that cut bloodlessly to the bone. Her mouth dry, Jazzy had no trouble believing that

Irene Baldwin would eliminate anything that stood in the way of her plans for her daughter.

Even a contest judge?

Her heart pounding, Jazzy couldn't help noticing the woman's size again. Broad, sturdy shoulders. Well-muscled arms. Jazzy's thumb rubbed almost absently across the fingers that had been crushed in those man-sized hands. Her pulse pounded like an overwound clock. Why had she sent that deputy back to the room ahead of her?

A familiar voice sliced through the tension between them.

"Jazzy!"

Jazzy's knees went weak.

ELEVEN

Derrick crossed the lobby toward the place where Jazzy stood talking with a tall woman. As he neared, the strain in her body became obvious. Her shoulders were rigid and one hand was clenched into a tight fist. Tension pulsed between her and the woman in nearly perceptible waves.

Wide green eyes turned his way, and there was no mistaking the relief they held. She was glad to see him! A burst of pleasure shot through him.

"There you are." Jazzy unfisted her free hand and hooked it through his arm. "I've been waiting for ages. What took you so long?"

Derrick played along with her game. "Sorry. I got tied up." Her hand trembled on his arm. She was really shaken up over whatever they'd been talking about. He covered her hand and pressed, then dipped his forehead toward the woman. "Good morning."

Strong lips tightened. "Morning." Her gaze slid to Jazzy for one last black look. "I'll see you this afternoon."

The woman's words lay between them, heavy with menace. She moved with long strides across the lobby toward the front desk.

Derrick watched her retreating figure. "Making new friends, are you?"

Jazzy went limp. "I've never been so glad to see anyone in my life. Thank you for rescuing me from that…that rabid pageant mother."

Understanding dawned. "Ah. I guess the word is out about the new judge."

"Apparently so, and not just about the pageant."

Confused, Derrick shook his head. "What do you mean?"

"The identity of the new barbecue judge has leaked out, too." She peered up at him with a curious expression. "You haven't heard?"

"Heard what?"

A shudder passed through her petite frame. "Do you mind if we sit down while I tell you about our, uh, eventful night?"

She extracted her hand, leaving his arm cold and missing her touch. A couple of upholstered chairs sat nearby in front of a big potted plant, and she headed toward them. Instead of following, Derrick put a hand on her back and steered her toward the restaurant.

"I could use a cup of coffee."

For a moment he thought she might refuse, but then she looked down at the cup she held. "I guess I could use a refill. Mine has gone cold."

As they stepped through the entrance, the savory smell of bacon stirred up a rumble in Derrick's stomach. He held up two fingers to the hostess, and they followed the woman to a booth in the back corner. Derrick refused her offer of a menu. "I'm on my way to my mom's for breakfast, so I'll just have coffee right now, thanks. Plenty of cream and a couple of sugars, please." He looked at Jazzy with a start. "I'm sorry. Did you want to order breakfast?"

She shook her head. "Just another coffee, please. Black."

When the woman left, Derrick folded his hands on the table and gave Jazzy an expectant look. "So I guess you didn't have a quiet evening in the room after all?"

Her chest jerked with a silent laugh. "The evening was pretty quiet, but it was all downhill from there."

Derrick listened to her describe the events of last night. Horror crept over him at the mention of the bottle of barbecue sauce the killer left behind.

When the server arrived, Jazzy fell silent. The woman set white cups and saucers in front of them and filled them from a pot. She placed a cream jug and a sugar dispenser beside Derrick's elbow.

When she walked away, Jazzy continued. "Sheriff Maguire didn't think the murder and the attack were related to the barbecue competition at all." She scowled, obviously not in agreement with the sheriff.

Derrick poured a third of the cream into his coffee. "So he thinks the sauce was meant to throw the police off the trail?"

"He seemed pretty sure about that at first. But when we realized last night's attack was an attempt to get Caitlin's camera, he might have changed his mind." Her lips warped into a crooked line. "At least, I think so. He clammed up pretty tight after that. I couldn't pry anything else out of him. He just kept telling me to leave the investigation to him."

Derrick swirled his spoon slowly through the tan liquid in his cup, stirring in a steady stream of sugar. "That sounds like him. He doesn't appreciate anyone trying to mess around in official sheriff's business."

A bit of coffee splashed over the rim into the saucer. Derrick licked the spoon dry, then picked up his cup for a sip. When he did, Jazzy folded her napkin and reached across the table to sop up the coffee in the saucer. Derrick hid a grin behind his cup. She really was the neat freak her friends accused her of being. She and his mother would get along great.

He took another sip, savoring the sweet warmth as it rolled

across his tongue. "So I guess that woman out in the lobby hadn't heard the news."

Jazzy tilted her head. "What do you mean?"

"Well, obviously you and your friends aren't going to judge now, not after last night."

"Of course we are. We said we would, and we're not the kind to back out of our commitments."

Disbelief stole over Derrick as he stared across the table. "Jazzy, nobody would blame you. In fact, once people hear that an attempt has been made on Liz's life, nobody will expect you to keep those commitments."

Jazzy's head tilted back as she lifted her delicate chin a stubborn fraction. "Even your sister?"

Derrick leaned against the rear cushion. Chelsea would be frantic to have the musicians back out just hours before the wedding. But they'd manage. If nothing else, he could draft old Mrs. Ingersoll to play the piano. She could probably still play if she took her arthritis medicine and he wheeled her chair up to the keyboard. "Chelsea would understand. I'll take care of it."

Green fire flashed in her eyes. "I don't need you to take care of anything. We're staying, and that's final."

Frustration sizzled along his nerve endings. Why wouldn't she listen to him? He was just trying to make sure she was safe. There was a murderer running around town, for crying out loud.

Derrick opened his mouth to make a stronger argument when a harsh voice snapped at him from across the restaurant.

"Derrick Stephen Rogers, what do you think you're doing?"

His spine stiffened to attention at the familiar voice from his childhood. He leaped out of the booth and stood with his arms hanging uselessly at his side as Aunt Myrtle stomped across the restaurant toward him. Her harsh expression defied anyone to question the necessity of the cane that pounded the floor with each step. As a boy, Derrick had developed a habit of giving that cane wide berth, since Aunt Myrtle was known to use the crooked handle to snag unsuspecting nieces or nephews as they passed by her chair. He and Chelsea had suspected that Aunt Myrtle wielded that cane as a weapon, not a walking aid.

"I told you on the phone to meet me in the lobby at *six forty-five.*" Steel-gray eyes bore into his. "Do you know what time it is?"

"Uh..." Derrick glanced at his watch and gulped. He was seven minutes late. "I'm sorry, Aunt Myrtle. I was here early, really. But I ran into a friend...." He gestured helplessly toward the booth.

Aunt Myrtle's stern expression transformed itself. Actual dimples creased her rouged cheeks as she bestowed a dazzling smile on Jazzy. She hooked the cane over her left arm and extended her right. "Well, hello. Aren't you a pretty girl? Myrtle Rogers, Derrick's great aunt from Sarasota. And your name is?"

A becoming blush bloomed on Jazzy's cheeks. She glanced at Derrick as she stood and took Aunt Myrtle's hand. "Jasmine Delaney. It's a pleasure to meet you, Mrs. Rogers."

"It's *Miss,* dear." The older woman covered Jazzy's hand with her other one, the cane dangling in midair. "I'm the old maid of the family."

Jazzy's smile deepened. "And you're in town for the wedding?"

"Yes, I flew in last night and had to take a *taxi* from the airport in Bowling Green." She *tsked* with disapproval. "The price I paid to get here! But nobody would come to pick me up. It seems they were all busy." The glance she threw toward Derrick was designed to inflict guilt, and she had it down to an art.

"I'm sorry," he mumbled. "We had the rehearsal."

Jazzy gestured toward their cups. "Won't you join us?"

"Heavens, no, dear. We don't have time. Didn't Derrick tell you?" Aunt Myrtle raised a gray eyebrow in his direction. "I'm to spend the day with Chelsea. There are a million and one things to do before the wedding. Hair, makeup, reception favors to make."

Derrick knew Mom would prefer not to have Aunt Myrtle underfoot all day, but the old lady was accustomed to having her way.

"Jazzy is one of the musicians for the wedding," Derrick told his aunt. "You should hear her play her fiddle."

A crease appeared between Jazzy's eyes. *"Violin."*

"Ah!" Aunt Myrtle threw her head back and assumed a look of ecstasy. "I love a good violinist. Do you play Pachelbel?"

Real delight overtook Jazzy's expression. "We do! In fact, we're playing "Canon in D Major" at the reception this evening."

"One of my favorites. Do you also know…"

Derrick listened with growing impatience as they spouted a bunch of foreign-sounding names at each other. None of it made a lick of sense to him. He glanced openly at his watch several times, and finally broke into Jazzy's animated description of some song or other with a Latin-sounding name.

"Aunt Myrtle, didn't you say you wanted to be at Mom's house by seven?"

The old lady started, then threw him a sour look. "It's your fault we're late." She turned her smile back on for Jazzy. "We need to leave, dear. I don't want to do anything to upset the bride on her wedding day."

Jazzy flagged down their server and ordered two coffees to go. Derrick threw a few dollars down on their table and then assisted Aunt Myrtle to the entrance. The server brought Jazzy's coffees as they reached the doorway.

"Aunt Myrtle, I'll be right back," Derrick told his aunt. "I want to make sure Jazzy gets back to her room okay."

Jazzy opened her mouth, probably to protest, but Aunt Myrtle cut her off with a shrewd smile. "Always the gentleman, our Derrick." She lowered her voice to a stage whisper and leaned close to Jazzy's ear. "I notice you're not wearing a ring, dear. He'd be a good catch."

Flames erupted in Derrick's cheeks. He studied the pattern on the worn lobby carpet while Jazzy bid the old woman goodbye with more self-possession than he could muster.

"I'll be right back," he mumbled to Aunt Myrtle.

Jazzy started toward one of the hallways at the rear of the lobby, and he shuffled alongside her. "Sorry about Aunt Myrtle."

She turned her head and smiled up at him. "I think she's delightful."

They rounded the corner. Derrick caught sight of one of Sheriff Maguire's deputies at the other end of the long hallway, a stark reminder of the danger Jazzy and her friends were in.

"Have you prayed about judging those—" he began.

She cut him off with a look. "We have. We're doing them. Discussion over."

Irritating woman. Derrick spoke through clenched jaws. "At least stay out of sight today. Don't make the deputies' job harder than it has to be."

She flashed him a look that might have been slightly less belligerent. "The pageant is right here in the hotel at three, so the only place we're going is your sister's wedding." They walked on for two steps. "Oh, yeah. And there's some sort of meeting Liz and Caitlin have to go to at noon to get instructions on judging tomorrow."

The sheriff would probably send a deputy with them. As long as they stuck together, they'd be okay. But knowing Jazzy, she'd probably do something foolhardy, like run off on her own.

"What are you going to do?" he asked.

She shrugged. "I don't know. Maybe stay here and practice a little."

She sounded hesitant, and no wonder. Who'd want to sit in

the same room where someone had broken in and tried to strangle her friend just hours before?

Months ago Derrick had scheduled the day off from his job at the power company in case Chelsea needed him to do something on her wedding day. But the thought of hanging around Mom's house and dealing with the bridesmaids, and the hair and makeup people, and Aunt Myrtle…

He made a snap decision. "Let me take you on a tour of the Bar-B-Q Festival route. It's right here in this area, all up and down the river. Give you a chance to stretch your legs."

They reached the door to her room. Her gaze did not rise from the cups as she handed them to him and extracted her key card from a back pocket. "I'd better not."

"Come on." He dipped his head to catch her eye. "It'll be better than sitting in that room all by yourself. And you can try some of Waynesboro's world-famous barbecue. I guarantee it's the best you've ever had."

The corners of her mouth tugged upward. "You guarantee it?"

"Absolutely."

The grin broke free. "Well, in that case."

Derrick's pulse skipped as she sliced the card through the door lock. She propped the door open with a foot, then took the coffee cups back from him.

He pulled his cell phone out of his pocket. "What's your number, in case I get tied up with wedding stuff?" He punched her number into his phone, then took a backward step. "So I'll pick you up in the lobby at a quarter 'till twelve."

Jazzy gave a single nod, then disappeared through the door.

His step light, Derrick turned and headed toward the lobby. Even Aunt Myrtle couldn't sour his mood this morning.

TWELVE

Jazzy let the door close and leaned against it until her pulse settled back into something resembling a regular rhythm. Totally ridiculous the way her stomach fluttered when Derrick asked to show her around the Bar-B-Q Festival. He wasn't at all her type. She'd established that already.

"There you are!" Caitlin rushed around the wall that formed a short hallway just inside the suite's door. "You've been gone so long we were starting to get worried."

Liz, fully dressed but still buttoning the top of her blouse, joined them from the bedroom. "After the night we've had, you could have at least left a note and told us where you were going." She relieved Jazzy of one of the cups and took a sip, her eyes closed with ecstasy. "Ah. You're forgiven."

"I'm sorry." Jazzy handed the other cup to Caitlin. "I figured the deputy would tell you."

"He did." Caitlin followed Liz to the sofa, Jazzy trailing behind. "We just got worried when you stayed gone so long."

Jazzy looked around the room. Her friends had straightened the place up in her absence. The sofa bed had been folded up, and Liz's suitcase lay in a corner with the contents neatly folded. Even the music and brochures on the desk had been straightened into orderly stacks. "Where's Matt?"

"He went home after we got up." Liz dropped onto one of the sofa cushions. "But he left two of his buddies, one for the front and one for the back." She jerked her head toward the patio door, which had been secured with a thick metal rod wedged horizontally against the opposite casing. Through the open curtains Jazzy glimpsed a uniformed man leaning against the outside wall.

She perched on the love seat, facing her friends. "I've had an interesting morning."

"Oh, yeah?" Caitlin, seated beside Liz, drew her legs up beneath her and directed her full attention toward Jazzy. "Tell us."

Jazzy described her conversation with Bradley, including the details of the missing security recordings and the fact that there were no external cameras that might have caught the intruder last night. Then she told them about being accosted—there was no other word for the encounter—by Irene Baldwin. And finally, she ended with Derrick and his Aunt Myrtle.

"So," she concluded, "I'm going to spend an hour or two with Derrick this afternoon while you two go to your meeting."

Liz and Caitlin exchanged shrewd smiles.

"What?" Jazzy asked innocently. "He's just trying to keep me occupied while you guys are busy, that's all."

"Right." Liz's smirk held more than its usual amount of sarcasm.

Caitlin's delight was more obvious. "He's so into you, girl. I think it's terrific. But what made you change your mind about him? Last night you said he wasn't your type."

"He's not." Jazzy paused, her unfocused gaze rising to the picture on the wall above her friends' heads. "But he said something that kind of caught my attention." She lowered her gaze first to Liz and then Caitlin. "He asked if we'd prayed about keeping our commitment to judge the contests."

Both their mouths formed amazed *O*'s.

"So the guy's good-looking *and* a Christian." Caitlin's grin was contagious.

Jazzy felt her lips trying to answer, and schooled them into a straight line. "I already knew he was a Christian, but his question says a lot about the depth of his faith. Still, that doesn't change the fact that he's really not my type. We have nothing at all in common. And besides, we live four hours apart. Not exactly an ideal dating situation."

"But…" Liz prompted.

Jazzy's top teeth bit down on her lower lip to keep it under control. "But it's just lunch and a walk. I mean, why not?"

"Exactly." Caitlin giggled, then she got serious. "You do have one thing in common though. A very important thing. You're both Christians. That's a pretty big factor, if you ask me."

Jazzy thought so, too. She'd made a commitment in Sunday school last year at the urging of her pastor's wife to prepare herself for the marriage the Lord had in store for her. That included only dating Christian guys. She'd been on three dates since then, all of them lukewarm on the romance thermometer. Her recent prayers had focused pretty intently on petitioning the Lord for a Christian boyfriend. For him to be husband material, she wanted the guy to enjoy the same things she did—concerts and foreign films and nice meals in elegant restaurants. Derrick seemed more like a hotdog-on-a-picnic-table kind of guy. Definitely not a candidate for a long-term relationship.

But a date was a date, and she intended to enjoy the hotdog. Or barbecue, as the case may be.

"You know," she said as a guilty flush warmed her neck, "I told Derrick we'd prayed about this whole contest thing, but we really haven't. I mean, I've shot up a few arrow prayers, but could we pray together?"

"Absolutely." Liz settled herself more comfortably on the sofa while Caitlin leaned forward to set her cup on the coffee table.

"You start," Caitlin said to Jazzy. "Then Liz, and I'll close."

Her heart full of gratitude for the friends God had given her, Jazzy bowed her head.

At eleven-forty Jazzy waved goodbye to her friends and Bradley as they exited the hotel on the heels of Deputy Frank. They would ride to the meeting at the VFW in the back of the deputy's cruiser. Sheriff Maguire was taking no chances with their safety, which went a long way toward relieving Jazzy's anxiety.

Her mood light, she selected a spot on the sofa near the front desk to wait for Derrick. The lobby was comfortingly busy. Dozens of conversations combined to form an indistinguishable clamor that echoed around her. The festival event marquee indicated that the Toddler Pageant had just ended, and the Youth Pageant began in twenty minutes, which explained the crowd.

A steady stream of mothers with young girls in Sunday-school clothes paraded in front of her, heading in the direction of the International Ballroom. A few even wore makeup, Jazzy noticed with gathering disapproval—the oldest of those girls was no more than six or seven. Another stream consisting of much younger children filed past in the opposite direction. She caught a few angry scowls on the faces of the parents, heard a few irate voices from both moms and dads. Apparently their kids had not won, and they didn't look happy about it. Did they blame the judges? Unease nibbled at the precarious peace she'd managed to establish.

At least she didn't see any sign of Irene Baldwin.

Forcing herself to relax, Jazzy settled more deeply into the sofa. The cushions were old and threadbare in places, but extremely comfortable. Her interrupted night's sleep was starting to catch up with her. She didn't bother hiding a wide yawn.

"I'm not keeping you up, am I?"

She looked up to find Derrick standing over her, a teasing grin aimed her way. He'd changed clothes from this morning, she noted, and the thought pleased her. His button-down shirt was a touch dressier than the T-shirt he'd worn earlier, but the brown plaid was still casual enough for walking around the festival. And it matched the color of his eyes almost exactly.

Embarrassed at the turn of her thoughts, she quipped, "Yes, but you're not doing a very good job of it. I was just about to doze off."

He glanced at his watch as she stood. "I'll have you know I'm right on time."

"And I'm glad, because I'm starving."

The continental breakfast they'd ordered from room service had lasted a few hours, but her empty stomach told her it was time for lunch.

"Then you're in luck. You're moments away from the best barbecue in the entire world, guaranteed."

Jazzy took the arm he offered. "You keep saying that. You realize you may be building up unrealistic expectations."

"Not a chance. You'll see."

They threaded through the people loitering around the lobby as he guided her toward the automatic doors. As they glided open, he said, "I hope you don't mind if we have some company. Old Sue loves the Bar-B-Q Festival."

Jazzy dropped his arm and stopped a foot inside the open doors. "You brought your dog?" She'd been about to add *"on a date?"* but bit the words off at the last minute.

"I hope you don't mind. The poor girl stays cooped up in my apartment all day long during the week while I'm at work. She won't be any trouble, though. I promise. There she is, right where I told her to stay."

Jazzy looked where he nodded. A dog sat on the sidewalk, its brown floppy ears perked forward. Its head moved as it watched the couple in front of them exit the hotel and head for the parking lot. At first glance Jazzy thought the animal was splattered with dirt. A second look showed her that the splotches covering the white body weren't dirt, but muted spots of brown fur. Brown also circled one watchful eye, making the poor thing look like she'd been walloped. Derrick's chest swelled as he smiled down at the creature.

"Oh, my." Jazzy cast around for something nice to say. It was definitely the ugliest dog she had ever seen. "She looks, uh, very obedient."

"She is. She won't move from that spot until I tell her it's okay. Isn't that right, girl?"

The last sentence was directed toward the dog with the affectionately indulgent tone Jazzy had heard some parents use with their children. Oh, no. He *was* one of those kinds of dog owners.

The dog had seen Derrick. An unbelievably long tongue lolled out of its mouth and its tail scraped back and forth across the concrete, but as Derrick said, it didn't move. He strode through the door toward the animal, and Jazzy followed hesitantly. Derrick stood straight in front of the dog and looked down at it. The tongue disappeared, and Old Sue's posture became crisp and unmoving.

"O-kay!" The moment Derrick said the word, the statue came to life and Old Sue rushed forward to receive an enthusiastic head-rubbing from her owner.

Jazzy hoped Derrick didn't expect her to touch the animal. The barbecue pits were all outside, so she might not have a chance to wash her hands before they ate. She shoved them into the back pockets of her jeans as Old Sue came forward to give her legs an enthusiastic sniffing. Actually, when the dog extended its neck, the disturbingly moist nose came up to belly-button level. Jazzy stood still and let the animal smell her.

Derrick watched, his expression amused. "You really aren't used to being around dogs, are you?"

"Caitlin has one. But it's much smaller." She didn't touch that one any more than necessary, either.

He started toward the parking lot, and Old Sue fell in beside him. Jazzy kept to the other side. She noticed the loops of a leash sticking out of Derrick's back pocket.

"You don't have to keep her on the leash?"

Derrick shrugged. "If anybody says anything I'll put it on. But she'll be okay without it."

When they stepped over the concrete barrier that outlined the hotel parking lot, the festival route stretched before them. Booths lined both sides of the street for several blocks, with wide gaps spaced intermittently on either side. Smoke billowed into the air from at least a dozen fire pits. The aromatic smell of burning wood and flavorful barbecue sauce blended to form the perfect appetite enhancer, and Jazzy's stomach gave a loud growl.

Derrick laughed. "Let's get some lunch in you. The only thing is, you have to try several different kinds of barbecue to get a true appreciation for Waynesboro's festival."

"Bring it on," she said. "I could eat a whole cow."

"You won't find much beef. The specialty hereabouts is mutton, but we do a lot of pork and chicken, too. Look."

They'd just come to the first of the giant fire pits. A row of enormous metal barrels cut in half stretched at least fifty feet long. They had been welded together, filled with wood and covered with yards of heavy grating. Row after row of huge chunks of meat lay atop the makeshift grills. Jazzy couldn't tell the pork from the mutton, but on the far side she saw what must be a hundred whole chickens. Heat miraged in visible waves as three men wearing bright green aprons basted the meat with sauce using long-handled mops. How could they stand that close?

Even from her vantage point ten feet away, the heat was almost unbearable. Meat sizzled as one man used a giant fork to flip a roast-sized chunk over, and the succulent odor that filled the air made Jazzy almost light-headed with hunger.

She grinned up at Derrick. "I'll try one of each. And burgoo, too."

"Oh, there's plenty of that. Did you see over there?"

Jazzy looked where he pointed. At the far end of the grill, two humongous metal cauldrons rested atop more blazing firewood.

"Wow." Jazzy hurried down the street to get a closer look. She had never seen pots that huge. She and Derrick could easily have stood inside along with Liz and Caitlin. Both containers were full almost to the brim with bubbling burgoo. A man stood beside one of them and stirred the simmering stew with an L-shaped wooden paddle. He smiled at Jazzy when he saw her watching.

"The best burgoo in the festival right here," he told her. "We've taken first place three years running."

"It smells wonderful." She looked up at Derrick. "Can we try some?"

"You bet."

He led her to an awning a few feet away. A man and a woman wearing green aprons identical to those of the cooks stood behind a long table. A big, shining trophy proclaiming "First Place Winner, Burgoo Competition" was proudly displayed on one end. Beneath it, a hand-lettered sign had been taped to the front of the table listing the prices for a cup of burgoo, or sandwiches of mutton, pork or chicken.

Old Sue sat patiently to one side, watching as Derrick placed their order. He balanced the three paper-wrapped sandwiches and two foam coffee cups filled with burgoo, and said to Jazzy, "You want to grab the drinks and some napkins?"

"Sure."

Beside the paper napkins was a basketful of Wet-Naps. With

a smile at the woman, Jazzy pocketed four and followed Derrick across the street. They dodged through a stream of festival-goers and slipped around the side of a big trailer that advertised funnel cakes for sale.

Waynesboro's Main Street ran alongside the river that Jazzy's hotel suite overlooked. A long stretch of deep green grass extended from the edge of the road down to the riverbank, with established old trees casting pleasant pools of shade. Stone picnic tables dotted the grass at intermittent positions, and Derrick headed for the first vacant one. Old Sue, apparently released from sticking close to Derrick's heels when her paws touched the grass, bounded ahead.

"How's this?" he asked when he reached his target.

Jazzy inspected the stone surface. "It'll be fine." Taking a paper napkin from the stack she carried, she brushed away an assortment of sticks and leaves, then unfolded two more napkins to act as place mats. She set a bottle of water on the corner of each, then positioned a plastic spoon on another folded napkin for each of them. She looked up from her work to find Derrick watching her with an amused grin.

"What?"

"Nothing." He shook his head and set a sandwich and a cup of burgoo on the napkin in front of her. "Just admiring the way you set a table."

Jazzy's cheeks warmed at his teasing tone, but she slid onto the bench without further comment. Instead of sitting down across from her, Derrick slid his makeshift place mat across the table and sat beside her.

At her questioning glance, he said, "That's a much better view." He nodded toward the river.

Jazzy had to agree, though she was surprised to feel a touch of disappointment that he didn't admit wanting to sit beside her.

Old Sue, apparently having inspected the river to her satisfaction, loped across the grass toward them and skidded to a stop beside Derrick.

"Yes, pest, I got you one, too."

"You did?" Jazzy raised an eyebrow. She'd assumed the third sandwich was for him.

"Old Sue loves mutton." He looked at the dog and commanded, "Sit."

Eyes fixed on the sandwich in Derrick's hand, Old Sue let her hindquarters drop to the grass.

"Watch this." He tore off a chunk of sandwich and set it on the bench beside him. "Wait for it," he told the dog. Old Sue froze, the only movement a twitching nose that hovered mere inches from the food. To Jazzy's amazement, the dog maintained its statuelike stance for much longer than she thought an animal's self-control would tolerate.

Not until Derrick said, "O-kay!" did Old Sue go for the food. Even then, she didn't wolf it down as Caitlin's dog would have done, but picked it up daintily and chewed before she swallowed.

"Why do you call her Old Sue? She doesn't look very old."

"I don't know. It just seemed to fit. But you're right, she's only three." Derrick tore off another chunk and extended it toward Jazzy. "You want to give it to her?"

Jazzy hesitated. She didn't really want to, but she hated to make a big deal out of her discomfort around dogs, especially when Derrick was obviously so fond of this one.

"I guess."

She took the piece of sandwich and held it between her fingers. Old Sue saw the transfer and shifted her position sideways, still sitting, to stop directly in front of Jazzy. She looked so funny Jazzy couldn't help laughing.

"She's very patient, isn't she?"

Derrick nodded. "She will sit there all day long if you make her."

Jazzy didn't want to torture the poor animal. She extended the food and said, "It's okay. You can have it."

Old Sue stretched her neck forward and gently took the bite. Jazzy felt no more than a brush of lips against her fingers.

"I've never seen a dog with such good manners," she told Derrick. "Let me give her some more."

Derrick handed her the sandwich and she fed it, a bite at a time, to the dog. When the sandwich was gone, Jazzy hesitantly lifted her hand to Old Sue's head and rubbed.

"Oh!" She looked at Derrick in surprise. "She's so soft. I thought her fur would be rough."

"I have a confession." Derrick ducked his head. "She got a bath this morning. I wanted her to make a good impression on you."

Jazzy turned her head toward the dog to hide the smile that curled her lips. She spent a moment stroking Old Sue's ears and marveling at the baby-soft fur. Then, with a final pat, she swiveled around on the bench. Fishing two Wet-Naps out of her pocket, she handed one to Derrick. "I'm sure she's clean, but still."

"Yes, ma'am."

They washed their hands, and then bowed their heads for a blessing. As Derrick started to pray, Jazzy realized she was enjoying herself far more than she would have thought possible a few hours ago. Why, she hadn't thought about the murderer for at least thirty minutes!

THIRTEEN

They spent the next hour sauntering through the festival, Jazzy stopping to check out a display of crafts beneath a colorful tent, or to watch one of the dozen or so competing teams cook their contest entries. She tried so many samplings of mutton, pork and chicken that her overfed belly strained at the waistband of her jeans. She had no problem conceding Derrick's claim that the barbecue at the Waynesboro festival was, indeed, the best she had ever eaten. Derrick bought hand-squeezed lemonade from one of the vendors who had set up booths along the street, and Jazzy sipped the sweet and tart liquid with relish.

The last of the displays lay at the elbow of a sharp right turn of Main Street, with a narrow alley running between tall brick buildings that marked the end of the festival route. Jazzy turned and looked back toward the Executive Inn at the far side. The street between the two end points was full of festival-goers following the path she and Derrick had just traveled.

"Let's walk back through the grass," Derrick suggested. "Give Old Sue a chance to stretch her legs."

Jazzy followed him to the parklike stretch of grass running alongside the river, laughing when the ecstatic dog bounded forward and back between the riverbank and Derrick. He set a slow pace, which Jazzy was happy to follow. She was not in any hurry to get back to the hotel. The closer they got, the more vividly the realization of the dangerous situation returned.

Derrick glanced at his watch. “What time do you need to be back for the pageant?”

Jazzy heaved a sigh. “Ten ’till three.”

“You don’t seem as eager to judge as you did yesterday.”

“I’m not,” she said truthfully. “I thought I’d get to judge the barbecue competition, or maybe the burgoo contest. But Caitlin and Liz volunteered for those, so I got stuck with this stupid pageant.”

“And you’re not as fond of pageants as you are of barbecue.” He watched her, his gaze shrewd. “Do you have some reason for disliking pageants? A bad experience, maybe?”

Jazzy walked a few steps before she answered. “Actually, yes. But not with a beauty pageant.” She looked up at him, suddenly shy. Oddly, she felt willing to trust him with a confession of something only her closest friends knew. “I have terrible stage fright.”

Surprise widened his eyes. “But you perform music in front of people all the time.”

She nodded. “I know. I’ve trained myself to keep the panicky feelings under control by losing myself in the music. And really, we don’t perform so much as accompany. At a wedding, for instance, everyone is looking at the bride, not at me.”

They took a few steps in silence.

“So did you always have stage fright, or did something happen to cause it?”

“I’ve had it as long as I can remember, to my mother’s great disappointment. I’m an only child, so I guess she didn’t have anyone else to pin her hopes on. She wanted me to be a performer, and whenever her friends or family came over she made me stand up in front of them and sing.” Discomfort churned in Jazzy’s middle as a handful of agonizing memories collided in her mind's eye. "I hated it. I even threw up once. But Mom insisted that the only way to conquer my fear was to confront it, so she kept pushing me to audition for plays at church or talent shows at school. I took up the violin because I figured playing an instrument in front of people would be a lot less scary than singing."

"And was it?" Derrick spoke gently.

Jazzy nodded, unwilling to look at him. She'd hate to see pity in his expression. "I guess it helped that I fell in love with the violin the first time I picked one up. And it turns out Mom was right. I still get nervous, but I haven't come close to throwing up in years."

"I'm really glad to hear that." His voice held a touch of amusement. "Chelsea wants a memorable wedding, but not in that way."

Their laughter lightened the memories of those fearful first years, and she turned a smile up toward Derrick. Old Sue loped toward them and shoved a nose into Jazzy's hand. Jazzy rejected the temptation to think about the number of germs that lurked in the wetness on a dog's nose, and obliged by rubbing Old Sue's ears as she walked. The dog enjoyed the caress for a moment and then dashed ahead.

"Anyway," Jazzy said in a lighter tone as she wiped her palm on her jeans, "I don't have anything against pageants in general, if the contestants are there because they want to be. But that mother this morning…" She gave a shudder. "You know, I've even wondered if maybe the sheriff should investigate the people associated with the pageant. I can totally see Irene Baldwin doing whatever it takes to make sure her daughter wins the Little Princess crown. She admitted as much to me."

Derrick screwed up his face. "I can't see that. I don't know the Baldwins, but I just can't imagine a beauty pageant would be so important to anyone that they'd commit murder."

Remembering Irene's determined glare, Jazzy wasn't so sure.

But she shrugged and turned a sheepish grin on Derrick. "I guess I've got baggage."

"We all have baggage," Derrick said.

Jazzy shot him a playful look. "Yeah? What's yours?"

He was silent for a few steps, his gaze fixed on a spot in the distance. "My baggage is full of stuff about my father's death, I guess. He got cancer when I was twelve and died three years later."

Jazzy sobered. Her mom and dad could be a bit overbearing and hard to take at times, but at least they were both still alive. "I'm so sorry, Derrick. That must have been tough for a teenager to handle."

"It was," he admitted. "But I have to say, he made sure those three years counted. He took me hunting or fishing every Saturday until he got so bad he couldn't get out of bed. And that last summer he insisted on watching every baseball game on television with me."

He fell silent as a loudspeaker intruded on their conversation, announcing the time of the horseshoe competition later in the afternoon. So his dad taught him to hunt and fish. No wonder he liked to do those things now.

Jazzy had wondered why Chelsea had asked her brother to give her away at her wedding. With the death of their father, Derrick had probably become the man of the house.

She stole a glance at his profile. No wonder he automatically assumed the role of protector when he sensed that Liz, Caitlin and she were in danger. He'd grown accustomed to taking care of the women in his life over the years.

Their path took them to a wide spot in the parklike strip of grass where a temporary stage had been erected. A lone man in denim overalls worked setting up folding chairs in neat rows facing the stage. Old Sue ran up to investigate the man, who stopped in his labor long enough to pat her on the head. Then he trudged toward a pickup truck that had been parked on the grass, its bed loaded with more chairs. Something about the man's slumped shoulders and shuffling gait tugged at Jazzy's heart.

"What in the world is he doing here?" Derrick asked.

She looked up to find Derrick staring at the guy. "Do you know him?"

He nodded. "That's Lester Kirkland."

Kirkland. Jazzy's eyes widened as the name registered. The brother of the man who was murdered. He must need money. She couldn't imagine any other reason someone would be working the day after his brother's violent death. "Is he very poor?"

Derrick lifted a shoulder. "No more than many around here." They drew close enough for a greeting, and Derrick called one out. "Hey, Les. How's it going?"

Mr. Kirkland's movements were slow as he turned toward them. He stood still, waiting as they crossed the few remaining steps. Jazzy searched the poor man's face. Heavy pouches of skin drooped beneath his eyes. The corners of his mouth pointed downward, though he didn't frown so much as his skin seemed to sag with sorrow. She recognized him from the church yesterday. The memory of his anguished cry when he learned of his brother's fate rang again in her ears, and she found it hard to look at him without letting her pity show.

"'Lo Derrick. Going good as can be expected, I guess." He shook Derrick's hand, but when his gaze slid to Jazzy he ducked his head to stare at his shoes.

"I'm Jasmine Delaney, Mr. Kirkland." She extended her hand. "I'm so sorry for your loss."

"Delaney." He glanced up once, then back down again. "You're the girl who found him."

She nodded. He released her hand after a quick shake and scuffed a toe in the grass.

"What are you doing out here, Les?" Derrick's gesture swept the even rows of chairs.

"They've got a bluegrass band coming at four. Gotta have a place to set up, don't they?"

"No, I mean why are *you* doing it? Surely the festival committee could have found someone else to take care of this today."

Mr. Kirkland shook his head. "I said I'd do it, and I aim to. Set up for your sister's wedding down at the church this morning, and now this. And later tonight I'm due over at the hotel to take down the chairs after the Miss Bar-B-Q Pageant." His gaze became unfocused as it fixed on the rapidly moving river behind the stage. "I gotta do something to keep busy. I'll go plumb crazy if I sit around."

Sympathy wrenched Jazzy's heart at the grief in the man's tone, an echo of his cry in the church. She laid a hand on his arm. "How is your mother doing?"

His lips twisted, and for one horrified minute Jazzy thought she'd made him cry. She removed her hand while he gained control of himself. "She ain't good. She's got a weak heart anyway, and I'm afraid this might do her in." He shoved his fists in the pockets of his overalls. "Josh was her youngest, and you know how a woman is about her baby. She was so proud of him she like to bust every time his name came up. Now he's gone, I don't know what she'll do."

"At least she still has you," Jazzy said.

He heaved a sigh. "I guess I'll be selling my trailer so's I can move back home and take care of her. She's got no business in that house up on top of that knob all by herself. She ain't got no neighbors. Nothing around but acres and acres of woods. If something was to happen to her…" He swallowed hard, shaking his head.

"Well, if there's anything I can do for her or for you," Derrick said, "you be sure to let me know."

"That's mighty kind of you. Thank you." Mr. Kirkland glanced into Jazzy's eyes, then quickly away. "I'm awful sorry you had to see that, ma'am. Sheriff said it was real bad."

After all he and his mother had been through, and the man was concerned for her. Jazzy swallowed back a lump that had gathered in her throat. "Please tell your mother I'll be praying for her. And for you, too, Mr. Kirkland."

FOURTEEN

The hotel parking lot was nearing capacity when they wove their way through the cars toward the entrance. Derrick tapped his thigh with a flat hand, the signal for Old Sue to heel. He was proud of the way she'd behaved herself in front of Jazzy today. And she seemed to have made an impression, too. He noticed Jazzy didn't use another Wet-Nap after she rubbed the dog's ears the last time.

"How many people come to this festival?" Jazzy asked.

"All told, about ten thousand."

Her jaw dropped. "You're kidding. That's probably more than the entire population of Waynesboro!"

He chuckled. "Not quite. Waynesboro has over twelve thousand residents, and about half again as many out in the county. But we do burst the seams during festival weekend, that's for sure."

They approached the automatic door and Derrick pointed to an out-of-the-way spot on the sidewalk. Old Sue trotted obediently to the place and sat. He looked her in the eye and commanded, "Stay."

A smile hovered around Jazzy's lips. "You've done an amazing job training her. Caitlin could use some pointers from you."

"I can't take much credit. She's a smart dog."

An air-conditioned breeze blew against them as they entered

the hotel. A little chilly for Derrick's taste. He placed a hand on Jazzy's back and guided her toward the hallway where her suite was located. Jazzy pulled her key card out of her back pocket as they crossed the lobby.

"You know what I've been wondering?" she asked, her voice low.

"What's that?

She stared thoughtfully at the card in her hand. "How did the killer get into that hotel room?"

Derrick had wondered the same thing. "He must have had a key, don't you think? The room was on the fourth floor. Too high to go through the window."

They turned down the hallway, and the noise from the lobby receded behind them. Near the stairwell at the other end, the deputy sat on a chair, speaking into a cell phone. He caught Derrick's eye, nodded and turned slightly before he continued talking.

"So how did he get it?" Jazzy asked. "Was the killer a hotel employee?"

Derrick shook his head. "I'm sure Sheriff Maguire is working on digging out the answer to that. He's probably questioning every employee who had access to a pass key."

"A pass key," Jazzy repeated as she stopped before the door to her suite. She held her card up and studied it through narrowed eyes. "Surely all the pass keys are secured somewhere. But how easy would it be to get a key to open that particular room? I mean, could someone just walk up and ask the front desk to give them one?"

Derrick saw where she was going. "I'm sure the sheriff is looking into that, too. It's not our concern."

She caught him in a gaze that sparked with emerald fire. "Aren't you the least bit curious?"

He really wasn't. Poking his nose into a murder investigation didn't hold the slightest appeal to him. But he saw by the stubborn tilt to her chin that Jazzy was going to follow through with this idea. And if she did, she'd better have someone there to watch her back. Now that was a job he could get into.

"Want to find out?" he asked with a grin.

He pulled his wallet out of his back pocket and extracted a credit card. He held his hand out for Jazzy's key, and when she gave it to him he pressed the two cards together. Counting off thirty seconds, he offered the key card back to her.

"Now you need a new key. Yours doesn't work anymore."

"Really?" She whirled around and slid the key through the lock on the door. A red light blinked.

Derrick grinned at her arched eyebrows. "A cell phone will do the same thing, but I left mine in my truck."

"Well, let's go see what we can find out."

They returned to the lobby and approached the front desk. The two desk clerks on duty were busy checking people in, so she and Derrick had to stand in line.

When their turn came, Jazzy whispered, "That's Emmy, the same girl who checked me in yesterday."

They approached the desk, and the teenager behind it asked, without looking up from her computer, "Can I help you?"

"Yes." Jazzy held the card toward her. "My key isn't working. Can I get a new one?"

"Room number?"

Jazzy gave it, and the girl typed it into her computer. Her extra-long fingernails made a tap-tap-tapping sound as they struck. Derrick couldn't imagine how she could type with those multicolored claws, but she seemed to manage.

She looked up at Jazzy. "Can I see an ID?"

"Oh." Jazzy splayed her fingers and cast a chagrined look at Derrick. "My purse is in the room."

Emmy softened. "It's okay. I remember you, Miss Delaney.

Mr. Goggins gave you and your friends keys to the owner's suite, so I'm sure it'll be fine."

She took the card from Jazzy and stepped sideways to an encoder machine with a numeric keypad and a small display screen on the front. Jazzy lengthened her neck and peered over the counter. She caught Derrick's gaze and nodded almost imperceptibly. Derrick looked where she indicated and saw an open box with what must be hundreds of key cards stacked neatly inside. The counter was low enough that he could easily have reached over and grabbed a handful. Could have reached the machine, too, if nobody was looking. He glanced upward at the camera suspended from the ceiling in the corner.

Emmy punched Jazzy's room number into the machine and slid the card through the encoder slot, then handed it back to Jazzy with a smile. "There you go."

As easy as that.

Jazzy started to turn away, but Derrick stopped her with a hand on her arm. "Can I ask you a question?" he asked Emmy.

Emmy nodded.

"When Miss Delaney checked in yesterday she was given another room."

"Four oh five seven," Jazzy said.

Emmy shuddered. "I remember."

Derrick figured none of the hotel employees would ever forget that number. "I was just wondering when the previous person checked out of that room."

A knowing expression came over the girl's features. "I wondered that myself, so I checked the computer to be sure." She glanced sideways at the older woman working behind the other monitor and lowered her voice. "That room has been empty for months. In fact, that whole hallway stays empty unless we have something big going on like the festival or a conference or something. We keep the AC turned off up there to save money."

Derrick nodded. Made sense. He doubted this place was ever filled to capacity except during the festival. He started to step away, but Jazzy tugged at his arm, her eyes fixed on Emmy.

"One more thing. When I checked in there was a woman complaining about the room she'd been assigned. You don't by any chance remember which room she was assigned to, do you?"

Emmy bit down on her lip while she thought. "Yeah, I remember her. She got all hyper with Stan." The girl's eyes went round. "I think she was checked into 4057 first, right before you. I remember when I swiped your card, the machine said the room was already occupied, but the computer said it wasn't."

Derrick put an arm on the counter and leaned over to check out the card encoder. A single cord ran from the machine to a power outlet. "I don't understand. You mean that machine isn't connected to the computer? They operate independently?"

Emmy gave an eye-roll. "This equipment is so old. The newer computers have everything all together, but we have to use this junk because we can't afford to upgrade."

Jazzy exchanged a loaded glance with Derrick before turning back to the girl. "So how do you know if a card has been made for a room already?"

"When I enter a room number, the card machine's display asks me how many days the guest will be staying. It keeps track of the number of days, so the card won't work after that. If I enter a room number that has active cards, it tells me somebody's already in there."

Derrick's pulse picked up the pace. "And when you swiped Miss Delaney's card yesterday, the machine told you the other woman was already in the room."

Emmy lifted a shoulder. "Not exactly. It told me there was

already a card active for that room. It doesn't keep track of names or anything. We have to look at the computer for that. But I figured it was the lady who was giving Stan such a hard time just then, because the computer said the room was free."

Derrick could see Jazzy's hands clenching and unclenching behind her back, but her voice betrayed none of the agitation she must be feeling. "Mr. Goggins told me this morning that there's nobody in 4057 now. But you gave me three cards for that room yesterday, and we gave them to the police. If you enter that room number into the machine, what would it say?"

Understanding dawned on Emmy's face. She rushed to the machine and punched in the room number. Her face was white with shock when she turned toward them after reading the display. "It says there are five keys active for that room. And two of them were made a week ago!"

FIFTEEN

Poor Emmy was staring at Jazzy like she was about to faint. "What should I do? Somebody needs to know about this."

"Don't worry," Jazzy assured the girl. "I'm going to call Sheriff Maguire right now. He'll probably want to talk to you."

Jazzy grabbed Derrick's arm and tugged him out of the way of the next person waiting in line.

"Let's go talk to that deputy right now," Derrick said.

They started across the lobby, but a familiar voice stopped them.

"Miss Delaney!"

She turned to see Bradley scooting across the lobby toward them, both hands extended. He grabbed Jazzy's and squeezed.

"Hello, Bradley. I wondered if you all would be back from the VFW yet."

Jazzy caught a small frown as it crossed Derrick's face. He was staring at their clasped hands. She hid a smile. Was he the tiniest bit jealous?

"Your friends are back in the suite, safe and sound." Bradley lifted his eyes dramatically toward the ceiling. "But the meeting was a fiasco."

"Oh, no! What happened?" Jazzy asked.

Bradley's glance darted around the lobby. The place wasn't

as crowded as this morning, but a good number of people loitered about.

"Come to my office." He let go of one hand and tugged her forward by the other. "I'd rather not talk about it out here."

Jazzy raised an eyebrow in Derrick's direction. Should they let Bradley in on their discovery? Since he was the manager of this hotel, she thought he should know. Derrick apparently agreed.

He gave a slight nod. "And we have something important to tell you, too."

Bradley's forehead creased as he looked up at Derrick. "That doesn't sound good. Come on in here."

Jazzy extracted her hand, and Derrick seemed to relax. They followed the manager past the front desk to a door marked Employees Only. He pushed through, and Derrick lunged forward to hold the door open for Jazzy. They entered a long, hall-like storage area. Wheeled racks for folding chairs took up a good bit of the space. Most of them empty. The chairs were probably all in use for the festival pageants. Against the back wall stood dozens of round tables. Jazzy had sat at similar tables during lunch meetings in other hotels. Wide double doors in the opposite corner must open onto the hallway right across from the International Ballroom. An old-fashioned punch clock hung on the wall to their right, and a time-card rack had been mounted beside it.

Someone had hand-lettered "Manager's Office" in white paint on a door beside the punch clock. The jingle of the keys Bradley extracted from his pocket echoed hollowly in the storage room as he unlocked the door and preceded them into the office.

He rounded a cluttered desk and collapsed dramatically into the chair on the other side. "Oh, you should have been there. It was terrible."

One visitor's chair was positioned across from Bradley, and

Derrick nodded for Jazzy to take it. She sat, leaving Derrick to lean against a long credenza on the side wall.

"We pulled into the parking lot the same time as Mr. Thompson, one of the other festival judges. Of course, he wanted to know why we arrived in a police car." Bradley tilted backward in the chair to stare imploringly at the ceiling. "Why couldn't we have gotten there five minutes later?"

Derrick folded his arms across his chest. "What did you tell him?"

"The truth, of course. That the sheriff had assigned a deputy to Miss Carmichael and Miss Saylor for their protection." Bradley's gaze bounced over to Jazzy. "Then Mr. Thompson ran inside and told the other judges about the attack on Miss Carmichael. All the judges of the barbecue competition wanted to know why *they* hadn't been assigned a guard, and then the burgoo judges started demanding that they were entitled to the same protection as the barbecue judges." He planted his arms on the desk and dropped his shaking head onto them. "They called Sheriff Maguire and insisted that he come immediately."

"How many judges are there?" Jazzy asked.

"Twelve. Three for each of the four trophies we award."

Four? Jazzy threw a silent question at Derrick, who ticked off a finger for each. "Mutton, pork, chicken and burgoo."

Bradley raised his head. "It's totally ridiculous the way they do this whole festival thing anyway, if you ask me. In my position on the festival committee I've tried to suggest a few ways to streamline." He slapped his chest flat-handed. "I served on the board of directors for the San Diego Art Festival. I have experience these yokels can't begin to match. But do they listen? Of course not."

Jazzy prodded the distraught manager back onto the subject. "So what did Sheriff Maguire say when he arrived?"

"He told them they had no reason to worry, that he was reasonably certain neither the murder nor the attack were in any way related to the festival. When they kept insisting that he assign them each a guard, he told them he'd have to deputize more men and the festival budget would have to cover the cost." Bradley's shoulders heaved in a silent laugh. "That shut them up. But the rest of the meeting was difficult." He raised a hand to his forehead. "It gave me a headache."

"I hope you have some aspirin," Jazzy said apologetically. "I'm afraid we're about to make your headache worse." She told him about their discovery of two extra key cards for room 4057. "So it looks like we found the reason for the missing security disks," she concluded.

Derrick nodded. "That card encoder is ridiculously easy to use, and it's within reach of anyone standing at the counter."

Bradley shot him a hurt look. "It isn't *ridiculously* easy to use. You didn't know how to use it until Emmy demonstrated. The average guest wouldn't have the slightest idea how to encode a key card."

"Unless they had experience from another hotel," Jazzy suggested.

"Or this one." Derrick leveled a hard stare on Bradley. "How much do you trust your employees?"

"If you're asking if I think any of them are capable of committing murder, the answer is no." Bradley drew himself up. "I pride myself on my ability to identify honest and trustworthy employees."

Derrick straightened and turned to face the credenza. From an open CD case on the edge he extracted a disk in a white paper sleeve and held it up. Jazzy caught a glimpse of dozens of identical CDs in the case. Yesterday's date had been scrawled across the front of the disk in Derrick's hand. "Then how do you explain the missing security disks? They're locked right here in this office, aren't they? Who has access other than your employees?"

Bradley sagged back in the chair. "I can't explain it. The sheriff asked the same thing. The only key to this office besides the one on my personal key ring is in a drawer at the front desk. The drawer should be kept locked, but..." He shook his head. "Any employee who goes back behind the counter has access to it."

"What was going on here last Friday and Saturday, anyway?" Jazzy asked.

"Nothing Friday. All day Saturday the Waynesboro Fish & Game Association had a tournament out on the river. They held the registration and kickoff in the International Ballroom. We had about seventy-five people in there Saturday for coffee and donuts at six in the morning."

Derrick nodded. "I was there. Just a regular meeting, nothing unusual."

"We have meetings like that fairly often," Bradley said, then went on with a touch of acid. "Nobody actually *stays* in this hotel, but they like to meet here."

"Well, something unusual must have happened that night, or the security disk wouldn't have been taken." Jazzy's toe tapped against the floor as she thought about those missing security disks. And the office key. And the extra cards encoded to room 4057.

She spoke slowly, organizing her thoughts as the words rolled off her tongue. "Okay, let's think about this. The killer would have to know how to use the card machine. That points to an employee of this hotel."

"Or maybe someone who is observant," Derrick said. "All he'd have to do is stand there and watch a couple of times to figure it out."

Jazzy conceded the point with a nod and went on to the next.

"He knows where the key to the manager's office is kept, and again, hotel employees know that."

Bradley winced, but nodded.

Jazzy continued. "He has access to the key, which means he can get behind the counter without being noticed. Again, an employee." She looked at Bradley. "Unless there's ever a time when the front desk is left unattended?"

Bradley started to shake his head, then stopped. "They're not supposed to ever leave the front desk unattended, but at night there's only one clerk on duty. The poor guy has to go to the bathroom sometime, doesn't he? But that's why we have the security camera running all night."

A slow smile spread across Derrick's face. "This is starting to makes sense. The killer comes in here late Friday night, waits until the clerk goes to the bathroom, swipes a couple of keys for a room that he knows is going to be empty all week and takes the key to the manager's office out of the drawer."

Jazzy shook her head. "No, that's not right. Why take the key then? He couldn't have gotten Friday night's security disk until it was out of the machine or Bradley would have noticed the next morning, right?"

Bradley nodded, but Derrick raised a hand.

"I'm not through yet. During the day on Saturday the guy makes a copy of the office key, and then Saturday night he again waits until the clerk goes to the bathroom to put the original back."

Understanding dawned for Jazzy. "So he had a spare key to get into this office—" she punched the desk with a finger "—any time he wanted all last week."

"That's right." Derrick switched his gaze to Bradley. "But that scenario still points to an employee."

Bradley sat with his eyes fixed on the desk in front of him. Slowly the creases cleared from his forehead. He sucked in a noisy breath. "Wait a minute. I know somebody else who was here last Friday night."

"Who?" Jazzy demanded.

The hotel manager stared at her with unseeing eyes for a long moment. Then his gaze focused and he shook his head. "No, I'm wrong. It doesn't make sense. I'm trying too hard to come up with someone who isn't an employee." He shot a pleading look first toward Derrick and then toward Jazzy. "I just can't believe any of my employees would commit such a terrible act."

The hard stare Derrick fixed on Bradley made Jazzy glad she wasn't the recipient. "If you know something, or even suspect someone, you need to tell the sheriff." His voice held more than a hint of warning.

But Bradley shook his head. "I'm not going to set the sheriff on…" He snapped his lips shut on whatever he was about to say, then went on. "On an innocent and unsuspecting person who doesn't deserve to be questioned by the police."

The phone on his desk beeped once. He punched a button, and Emmy's voice filled the small room.

"Mr. Goggins, a guest out here is asking to see you. She says there's not enough light in her bathroom—"

"Not *nearly* enough," insisted an obstinate female voice in the background. "How anyone can be expected to get ready for a pageant in that flat light is beyond me."

Bradley's eyelids flickered shut as he inhaled a long, slow breath through his nose. "Please tell the guest I'll be right with her." Hands flat on the desk, he pushed himself out of the chair. "Duty calls, I'm afraid."

"But if you—"

He thrust a palm toward Jazzy to silence her protest. Frustrated, she jumped to her feet and preceded him out of the office.

* * *

Back in the hotel lobby, Jazzy made for the back hallway, but Derrick stopped her.

"I'll walk you back to your room, but first I'd like to check on Old Sue. She's been out there quite a while."

Jazzy gasped. "Poor Old Sue! I totally forgot about her."

They headed for the entrance and passed two giggling girls with their hair in curlers. Probably contestants for the Little Princess pageant. Jazzy followed Derrick, but when the doors swished open, Jazzy stopped dead in her tracks. She brought a hand to her mouth to cover a laugh.

Old Sue, well-trained and faithful, sat vigil in the exact spot Derrick had left her. But apparently some of the pageant kids, presumably the girls they'd just passed, had noticed the docile animal and decided to pretty her up. Someone had fastened a gigantic yellow hair bow with red polka dots onto her collar, and a smaller violet one at the base of her tail. A red plastic barrette clasped the longish hair above each ear, and glitter sparkled on the spotted white fur down the length of her back.

Openmouthed horror stole over Derrick's features as he stared down at his hunting dog. "What happened to you, girl?"

The dog's tail went into action at the sight of her master, sending a shower of glitter onto the sidewalk. At the look on Derrick's face, Jazzy couldn't contain her mirth. She doubled over, resting her arms on her thighs as laughter overtook her.

"Surely you don't think this is funny." Derrick gave her a pained look. "How can you laugh at her humiliation?"

He started to remove the bow, but Jazzy stopped him.

"Wait! I've got to get a picture first."

Still giggling, she reached into her jeans pocket and dug out her cell phone. She flipped the lid open and pressed the button to activate the camera.

"Smile, Old Sue."

The phone *chuck-chucked* as it snapped a picture. The sound triggered a memory, and Jazzy froze. A white-hot thread of alarm wove its way through the fabric of her mind.

She whirled toward Derrick, eyes wide.

"What?" he asked. "Is something wrong with your phone?"

She shook her head, her breath coming quick. "I totally forgot something really important."

She punched the buttons on her cell phone to bring up the pictures stored in memory. The last shot she'd taken was in the hotel lobby when they were checking in.

"There." She studied the tiny screen. Hard to be sure, but a familiar if blurry figure stood behind Caitlin's frowning face. Jazzy shoved the phone toward Derrick. "I took that picture yesterday."

Her icy fingers trembled, and Derrick steadied her hand with his warm one. "It's not a very attractive shot of Caitlin, is it?"

"Not that! Look in the background. Do you know who that is?"

Derrick shook his head.

"Well, I do. We've got to call Sheriff Maguire." The blood seeped from Jazzy's brain as realization set in, leaving her cold and light-headed. "I don't think that intruder was after Liz last night. I think the intended victim was me."

SIXTEEN

"That is Irene Baldwin." Jazzy plastered on her most stubborn glare and directed it toward Sheriff Maguire. "I think she's the killer."

The sheriff stood in the center of their suite and sucked his cheeks in as he stared at the tiny screen on her cell phone. His mouth took on the shape of goldfish lips. "It's not a very clear picture. And what's that in the other corner?"

The others stayed back, unwilling to come between Jazzy and Sheriff Maguire. Liz sat on one end of the sofa while Derrick perched on the arm at the other end. He had brought Old Sue inside through the back entrance, and Caitlin knelt on the floor beside the dog, plucking glitter out of her fur.

"It's one of those big potted plants or something. The screen is too small to see well. But that's Irene." Jazzy wanted to stomp her foot, but instead of a blatant display of temper she settled for tapping the screen with an urgent finger. "I recognize her. And right about the time I snapped that photo was when she barged through the line to go up to the front and complain about her room. She'd probably been upstairs killing Mr. Kirkland minutes before then."

"With her daughter in tow?" Liz sounded skeptical.

Jazzy whirled to level a glare on her friend. "Maybe she told her daughter to wait in the lobby while she checked out the room. Or maybe Heidi did see something. You saw how upset she looked. She was all flushed."

"But how would Irene get Mr. Kirkland up to that room?" Caitlin asked.

"I don't know. That's his job to figure out." Jazzy pointed at the sheriff, whose expression remained stoic.

Liz spoke with more restraint than she normally used. "Tell me again why she would kill him."

Jazzy was about to answer when Derrick spoke up. "When I saw her this morning she had Jazzy cornered." He looked at the sheriff. "She did seem awfully determined that her daughter win this pageant."

Jazzy shot him a smile, then continued to plead her case with Sheriff Maguire. "Maybe she saw me snap this picture and she broke in here looking for my cell phone instead of Caitlin's camera. Liz and I both have dark hair—maybe she thought she was attacking me instead of Liz. When Liz woke up and started struggling, she saw she had the wrong girl and left."

Sheriff Maguire continued to stare at the phone, but his expression became thoughtful. Encouraged, Jazzy plowed on with her theory. "If the desk clerk checked her into room 4057 first and gave her two key cards, she had access to the room. Has anybody told you how long it was between the time she first checked in and when she came back down and demanded that they change her room?"

Caitlin didn't give him a chance to answer. "If she just checked in yesterday, how come the desk clerk said two of those key cards were made last week?"

Sheriff Maguire's eyebrows arched expectantly, waiting for Jazzy to answer. Thoughts shuffled through her brain as she tried to come up with a plausible explanation. "Okay, what about this?

Irene came to the hotel last Friday night and made the keys." As another puzzle piece fit into place, she snapped her fingers toward Derrick. "Bradley must have seen her here Friday. That's why he was reluctant to tell us who he suspected. He wouldn't want to accuse a hotel guest unless he was really sure. Then, when she actually checked in yesterday, she was shocked to be put in the same room she'd just committed a murder in. Or maybe—"

Sheriff Maguire cut her off with a scowl. "I understand your concern, Miss Delaney, but there is no compelling reason to believe this woman killed Kirkland. Nor does it seem she had the opportunity or the motive. No matter what you and Derrick say, I can't believe a little girl's beauty pageant is a strong enough inducement to commit murder."

"Parents will do all kinds of unreasonable things to see their children succeed," Jazzy insisted. "Don't you remember that case about the cheerleader a few years ago? A mother killed another mother because she thought it would upset the woman's daughter so much she would drop out of the tryouts. Then her daughter would have a better chance of getting on the squad."

Sheriff Maguire stood firm. "That was a unique situation, and that woman was obviously deranged. You're grasping, Miss Delaney."

Jazzy opened her mouth to protest, but then she closed it again. She was grasping. She realized it. But every time she closed her eyes, the gruesome image of Josh Kirkland's body sent a shudder rippling down her spine. A voice kept whispering in her head that Irene Baldwin was the murderer.

And that Jazzy might be the next victim.

She just needed to figure out how the woman had accomplished the act. If she could come up with a plausible scenario, the sheriff would have to take her seriously.

Sheriff Maguire snapped the cover of her cell phone shut.

"Regardless, I'm going to have to confiscate your phone. We'll let the experts have a go at that picture and see what they can come up with. Deputy Farmer will give you a receipt."

"But I don't have a land line at my apartment," Jazzy protested. "How long will it be before I get it back?"

The sheriff pocketed the phone and lifted a shoulder. "Shouldn't be more than a week or two. Same as Miss Saylor's camera."

She opened her mouth to complain, but closed it again in the face of the sheriff's stony expression.

"Fine," she mumbled.

She only hoped Irene found out that Sheriff Maguire had her cell phone with the picture on it. If Irene knew that, she just might let Jazzy make it through the next twenty-four hours—alive.

SEVENTEEN

The sheriff announced his intention to question Bradley, and left the suite. Derrick closed and latched the door behind Sheriff Maguire and Matt, who would relieve the other deputy at the end of the hotel corridor. He turned to find three anxious pairs of eyes fixed on him.

His obligation to these girls weighed heavily on his conscience. If he hadn't been so determined to find a classical music group to lend a touch of elegance to his little sister's wedding, they would be safe in their homes up in Lexington. He'd dragged them down here and plunged them into the middle of a dangerous situation that had already hurt one of them and had scared all of them nearly to death.

Misgiving wormed through his gut, leaving an aftermath of fear in the trail it furrowed. He wasn't at all sure this ordeal was over with. If only he could stick around…but this was his sister's wedding day. He'd already missed most of it, and he had duties to perform. He needed to get over to the house and be the big brother.

Lord, I feel responsible for them. What can I do to keep them safe?

An idea sprouted to full bloom in his mind. Whether from a divine source or his own need to protect these three, he didn't know. But he decided to go with it.

"Okay, listen up," he announced. "I've got to go play chauffeur for a bride and a whole passel of bridesmaids. But I'm going to leave Old Sue here. I'll come back at five o'clock to pick you up and take you to the church. Until then, I want you to stay together."

"Old Sue is a guard dog?" Jazzy eyed the animal, skepticism painted across her face. Aware that she was being talked about, Old Sue swept the floor with her tail, looking like anything but a fierce guard dog.

"She's never had to be," Derrick admitted. "But I think if she saw someone being attacked, especially someone she knows I like, she'd defend them. I really think it's best if she stays here with you."

Two heads nodded obediently, but Jazzy's spine stiffened and her eyes flashed across the room in his direction.

Honestly, that woman was as obstinate as they came.

"You don't have to leave your dog to guard us," she snapped. "We're surrounded by deputies. We have plenty of protection without Old Sue."

Worry drew lines across Caitlin's forehead. "What about when you go down to the pageant, Jazzy? If a deputy goes with you, that leaves us with one door not guarded. And if we all go, that leaves the suite unguarded. Someone could sneak in here and wait for us to return."

"Old Sue will wait here while you're gone," Derrick said.

Jazzy ignored him and whirled on Caitlin. "Now who's being paranoid? Go ahead, Liz. Tell her we don't need the dog."

Derrick hid a smile when Liz gave Jazzy an apologetic grimace. "Sorry, Jazz. Too much weird stuff is happening. I'd feel better with the mutt here."

Derrick watched the struggle on Jazzy's face. He had never met someone so all-fired eager to reject an offer of help. Maybe her determination to remain self-reliant came from being an only child. Wherever it came from, it was time she let go of it and accept what little protection he could give her.

He stepped forward and tried to place a hand on her arm, but she twisted away. His limp hand fell to his side. "Would you listen to me for one minute, please? I've been thinking about something that apparently hasn't occurred to you."

The hard line of her jaw slackened as a wary shadow darkened her eyes. "What?"

"All that stuff about the key cards and knowing which rooms would be empty and all that? I don't care what Bradley Goggins says, it all points to a hotel employee."

"Yeah, so?"

"So what if Bradley is right? What if the killer isn't one of his employees?" Derrick lowered his voice. "What if it's him?"

"No!" Jazzy shook her head so violently her short hair whipped around her ears. "That's ridiculous. Why would he want to kill Josh Kirkland?"

Derrick lifted a shoulder. "Kirkland had a pretty strong voice on the festival committee, and you heard Bradley. He's obviously gone up against the committee a time or two, and he's bitter about it. Maybe the two of them had words and things got out of hand."

Liz spoke up. "And then he dumped barbecue sauce on the body to throw suspicion onto one of the competitors, just like the sheriff said."

"Could be." He faced Jazzy squarely. "He definitely had access to the room, the keys, the security disks. Everything. Personally, I think he's a more likely suspect than that pageant mother."

Jazzy wrapped her arms around her middle. Her knuckles whitened as they gripped her arms. "I don't believe it." But her voice sounded less certain than it had a moment before.

Jumping on her hesitation, Derrick plowed forward. "Maybe I'm wrong. Maybe it was someone else, even Irene Baldwin. But one thing's certain. The killer has access to this hotel. And he thinks you ladies—" he let his gaze sweep all three of them "—have something that can identify him. Or her. Don't turn down an offer for a little added protection."

Derrick watched as Jazzy exchanged a glance first with Liz and then Caitlin. The expression she turned his way held resignation. His taut muscles loosened when she gave a single nod.

"I can't believe I'm doing this," Liz mumbled as she stomped down the hallway between Jazzy and Caitlin. "First you guys drag me down here to do a wedding gig in *Deliverance* country, and then I end up spending my Friday afternoon watching a bunch of miniature Miss Americas prance around in swimsuits and high heels."

Jazzy didn't bother to hide her amusement at her friend's trademark grumpiness. "I highly doubt they'll have a swimsuit competition in the Little Princess pageant."

Actually, Jazzy didn't blame Liz for her foul temper this afternoon. She had mentally kicked herself a dozen times in the past hour for insisting that they follow through with their commitment to judge these contests. Her second big mistake in as many days. If she hadn't, they could hang around the suite until the wedding, play the music they'd agreed to play and then go home. Forget the idea of the murderer following them. He—or she—seemed content to center his activity around this hotel. Now that Sheriff Maguire had Caitlin's camera and Jazzy's cell phone, Jazzy was becoming more and more certain that when Waynesboro receded in their rearview mirror, they'd leave the killer and the danger behind. The thought made her long for the solitude and safety of her apartment.

Derrick's crazy idea refused to quit bugging her. Bradley did have access to every single element needed to pull off the crime.

And Jazzy had to admit that he didn't seem to like anyone associated with the festival very much. The specter of the shadowy figure in the picture haunted her, too. Was it a person or a potted plant? It *might* be a person. But surely Bradley wouldn't care about being caught on camera. Nobody would question his presence in the lobby of his own hotel.

Her heel caught the hem of her silken black slacks, and she hitched up the flared legs. They'd all dressed in their formal wear for the wedding, since the pageant would end just moments before they needed to leave. A barrage of voices and laughter grew louder as they neared the end of the hallway. Matt, the deputy assigned to accompany them, scooted a little closer when they turned the corner into the lobby.

"Wow." Caitlin's eyes rounded as she took in the horde of people crowding the spacious lobby. "Where did they all come from?"

A long line wound its way from the front desk around the bank of elevators. Another cluster of people hovered at the entrance to the gift shop. Every chair had been claimed as people loitered about, chatting. Were they waiting for the start of the Little Princess pageant? Jazzy gulped. Or maybe they were out-of-towners, just arrived for a weekend of barbecue and burgoo.

Jazzy remembered what Derrick had told her earlier. "I guess the Bar-B-Q Festival draws a pretty big crowd."

"Thousands." Matt's voice came from comfortingly close behind Jazzy's ear. "And since the Executive Inn is right here at the end of the festival route, everybody wants to stay here. But this is nothing. Just wait till you see Main Street tonight." His uniformed arm extended between Jazzy and Liz as he pointed toward the far end of the lobby. "Let's make our way around the edge past the lounge. I don't want to lose you in the crowd."

They marched in the direction he indicated. The noise from

dozens of conversations assailed Jazzy's ears. Was one of the people in this lobby a murderer? Paranoia pressed in on her like a tightly coiled rope. The flesh on her bare arms crept. She had that feeling again—was she being watched? She scanned the faces of the people they passed.

Suddenly her gaze snagged on a pair of eyes staring directly at her.

Shock interrupted her heartbeat as she caught the menacing glare of Irene Baldwin. Jazzy grabbed Liz's arm in both of hers and hissed, "There she is! Irene. She's staring at me."

"Where?" Liz placed a comforting hand over Jazzy's. When she caught sight of the woman Jazzy pointed out with a nod, she sucked in a breath. "She's one scary-looking woman."

"You two quit it," Caitlin scolded. "She's not scary at all." She paused, staring. "Though she does look strong, doesn't she?"

"Exactly. Look at the size of her hands." Jazzy's words came out in a hiss, and Liz's fingers rose with an absent gesture to hover around her throat.

Matt placed a warm hand on Jazzy's shoulder and another on Caitlin's to steer them toward the wall. "Just keep on going. There's nothing to be worried about. I won't let anything happen to you."

Jazzy walked in the direction he indicated, but Irene seemed intent on speaking with her. The woman cut diagonally across the lobby to intercept them, each long stride loaded with purpose.

As she neared, Jazzy remembered the cell phone. When Irene discovered that Jazzy no longer had possession of the cell phone with the incriminating picture, the threat would be removed. She would be safe. She straightened her shoulders and stopped to wait for the woman to cover the last few feet between them.

"What are you doing?" Liz grabbed her arm and tugged, but Jazzy shook her off and held her ground.

"Good afternoon, Mrs. Baldwin." Jazzy was proud of her steady voice. At least the loose legs of her slacks hid the trembling in her knees.

"Afternoon." Irene nodded toward Liz and Caitlin. Her gaze halted for a moment on Matt before returning to Jazzy. "I heard you'uns had some trouble last night."

Jazzy hesitated. Why would Irene admit knowing about the attack? She glanced at the deputy before nodding.

"It's like I said." Irene's head shook side to side. "People in this town don't like outsiders coming in and messing up their plans."

Matt stepped forward, and Jazzy fought against the urge to edge behind his strong form. "Ma'am, if you know something about the attack that occurred here last night, you need to tell me about it. Whatever information you have might be important to an ongoing murder investigation."

Irene reared back, shock apparent on her face. "Murder?" She spat the word as though she couldn't stand the taste of it in her mouth. "I don't know nothing about that. But I told this gal this morning how much stock some people put in these here pageants. Pride is a terrible sin, makes people do terrible things."

"Well, just so you know, the police took my cell phone." Jazzy lobbed the news with all the finesse of a brick through a windshield. "They think there might be a picture stored in memory that will help them identify the person who killed Mr. Kirkland."

Her hopes for an incriminating reaction were disappointed. Irene's face remained stonelike. "Be that as it may, you just make sure you give a honest judging today."

The accusation stung. Was the woman actually accusing her of dishonest practices? Jazzy drew herself upright. "I am always honest."

They stared at one another, Jazzy unwilling to tear her gaze away until Irene did first. The woman's eyes slitted, and she gave a nod. "Long as we understand each other."

She started to turn away when Jazzy stopped her. Now would be a good time to verify their theory about the timing of the key cards. "Did you happen to come here, to this hotel, last Friday? At night, maybe?"

Irene's eyes jerked as her gaze darted sideways toward Matt and back again. "Ain't nothing wrong with that. It's allowed."

The noisy gasp Jazzy drew was echoed by Liz. Beside her, Matt's spine stiffened. "Mrs. Baldwin, if you were in this hotel last Friday night, that makes you a person of interest in this investigation. I'm afraid we're going to have to ask you some questions."

Fear flashed in her eyes. "I didn't do nothing wrong. My girl, she gets nervous is all. She wanted to see the place. Get a feel for it." The gaze she turned back on Jazzy held a hint of pleading. "You understand how it is."

Jazzy understood, all too well. She felt Caitlin's and Liz's eyes on her. They'd both accompanied her on advance trips to scout out a venue and get her bearings before the actual performance. It took the edge off of her stage fright if she was at least familiar with the place.

Probably reacting to the fear in the woman's voice, Matt softened visibly. "You're not being accused of anything, Mrs. Baldwin. But you may have seen something Friday night that will help us with our investigation. Sheriff Maguire is going to want to talk to you."

Irene's throat convulsed as she stared at the deputy. Jazzy felt her certainty crumble like a clump of dry dirt. If this woman was guilty of murder, wouldn't she have denied being here last week?

"Can it wait till tonight?" Irene's voice took on a tone of pleading. "The pageant's fixing to start, and my Heidi..." She paused, her gaze dropping to her feet. "She can't do her best without her mama there to cheer her on."

Jazzy knew how that was, too. A vivid memory flashed into her mind. Her mother seated on the second row of folding chairs in the school gymnasium, nodding encouragement to a terrified Jazzy, who did her best to make it to the end of "When You Wish Upon a Star" without throwing up. Even though Mom had forced her to enroll in the stupid talent show to begin with, her proud smile had given Jazzy the encouragement she needed to plow through to the end.

Matt glanced at his wristwatch. "Will you be around later, ma'am? Sheriff Maguire has a wedding to go to."

Irene nodded and gave him her room number to pass on to the sheriff. Her manner as she left was that of a woman who had been granted a reprieve.

"I don't think it was her," Caitlin announced as they continued on their way.

Liz shook her head. "I don't know. Her being here the night the first missing security disk was recorded is a pretty big coincidence."

Jazzy remained silent as she followed her friends to the International Ballroom to receive her briefing as a pageant judge. So many conflicting emotions sparred in her mind she didn't know what she thought anymore. About Irene *or* Bradley.

EIGHTEEN

"And another reason I want to be a doctor is because I think it would be good to go to places where the people are poor, like France. I'd like to go to France." The beribboned girl on the stage dimpled first at the three judges and then at the audience. Her smile wilted, and she stammered, "Uh, I mean like Africa. Or, or, uh, Kansas City."

Fighting hard to school her smile, Jazzy glanced into the audience in time to see a stern-faced woman in the second row give a slight nod of approval. The girl's dimples returned, and she executed a Shirley Temple curtsy before parading back down the runway to the rear of the stage.

Jazzy paused in her writing to clap a few times, then scribbled a final number on the bottom of the score sheet. Beside her, judge number two, whose name she had forgotten within seconds of hearing it, wrote a laborious paragraph at the bottom of her contestant feedback form. When the woman had been introduced to the audience, Kate—the pageant organizer and emcee—identified her as the owner of the local tanning salon. Jazzy would have guessed her occupation without being told by the deep bronze color of the woman's leathery skin. Jazzy considered putting on the sweater that hung over the back of her chair, just to hide the white of her arms, which surely looked sickly in comparison.

Beyond Tan Woman, the third judge sat with her folded hands resting on her rather large stomach, staring toward the gap in the curtain through which the next contestant would waltz when her name was called. Judge number three's claim to fame was a close family tie to Kate. She shared many qualities with her sister, including build and, unfortunately, fashion sense. The 2XL Hawaiian-print shirt put Jazzy in mind of vast floral fields pictured in tulip catalogues from Holland.

Jazzy's entire body tensed as her gaze slid toward the audience. If she'd known that she would be sitting at a table situated parallel to the runway in full sight of every person in the packed ballroom, she would certainly have refused this assignment. She'd figured the judges would be seated in the front row facing the contestants, not sharing the stage with them. The weight of hundreds of pairs of eyes was heavy on her. She'd been caught in many hopeful glances by a pageant mother, and more than a few meaningful glares. Thank goodness for Liz and Caitlin seated beside Matt in the front row, near enough to encourage Jazzy with smiles and nods. Though judging by the way the deputy slouched in his folding chair, he'd rather be anywhere than at a beauty pageant.

Yeah. Join the club.

Jazzy's gaze slid to Irene. Easily noticeable because of her hulking height, she sat four rows back on the end closest to the judges. Several times in the hour since the beginning of the pageant, Jazzy had looked up to find Irene's glower fixed on her.

Like now.

Jazzy turned her attention back to the stage as Kate introduced the next contestant.

"And next we have Miss Heidi Baldwin."

The girl edged between the curtains and turned toward the audience. Her brown hair cascaded over her shoulders in too many unnatural ringlets that spoke of hot rollers and tons of styling gel. The stage lights sparkled on a bright red bow at the back of the poor girl's skull that looked more like a Fourth of July centerpiece than headwear. Unfortunately, it matched her dress. For a long moment, Heidi froze. Her overround eyes screamed her terror as she stared toward the hundred or so faces turned her way. Jazzy's stomach roiled in an agony of sympathy.

Kate continued reading her introduction, oblivious to the girl's petrified state, though she stood behind a podium on the opposite end of the stage and could see perfectly well that Heidi was gripped by an iron fist of panic. But just as Jazzy thought the girl would collapse under the strain, she snapped out of her frozen fear and realized the introduction was her cue to walk the runway. She did, in small, mincing steps that bore evidence to the fact that she was unaccustomed to high heels.

Poor kid. Who would put high heels on a twelve-year-old anyway? Especially those hideous red ones that looked as if they ought to be tromping down the yellow-brick road?

Jazzy found herself whispering a mental prayer for the poor girl, and when the petrified gaze slid her way, Jazzy smiled broadly. Heidi, obviously terror-blind, didn't seem to notice.

Kate's introduction ended fifteen seconds before Heidi reached the microphone at the front of the stage. Those fifteen seconds were some of the longest of a very long afternoon as Jazzy listened to the sounds of the girl's shoes shuffling along the platform. The mic stood directly in front of Jazzy's seat, so she easily saw the stage lights glinting off tears that glistened on the gentle curve of the cheek closest to her. Jazzy shut her eyes in remembered agony.

The girl took a deep breath. "Hi—I'm—Heidi—Lynn—

Baldwin—and—I—want—to—be—an—actress—like—Angelina—Jolie—when—I—grow—up—so—I—can—make—a—lot—of—money—and—help—people—who—need—help—thank—you."

After a graceless but relieved turn, the girl practically flew down the long runway and escaped behind the curtain.

Jazzy hid her disappointment behind a schooled expression. She'd so hoped Heidi would earn a high score, and not just because of her mother's domineering insistence. But in good conscience, Jazzy couldn't award that performance more than a few points for having the courage to complete it. She could, at least, write an encouraging note on her feedback form applauding the girl's bravery. Maybe Heidi would do better in the talent component.

As she bent over her score sheet, Jazzy felt the curious burning sensation of a pair of eyes fixed on her. She couldn't help herself. She turned her head and locked gazes with Irene Baldwin.

If she were awarding points for poisonous glares, Irene would get a hundred.

Derrick hovered in the kitchen, the only place in Mom's house that wasn't overrun with giggling females. A couple of girls from the local beauty school had set up shop in the living room, and Chelsea's bridesmaids were taking turns having their hair turned into a mass of ringlets. How they could sit still while someone twisted chunks of their hair around a hot poker was beyond him. It stank of burning hairspray in there.

But that was better than the stench of nail polish that permeated the family room. A woman with sketched-on eyebrows had taken over the place, and was in the process of smearing gunk on Chelsea's face. When he stepped in there, the makeup woman had the nerve to suggest that a touch of powder would tone down his "ruddy complexion," whatever that meant. When he saw

Chelsea studying his face with a thoughtful expression, he beat a quick retreat. There were limits to what he'd do for his sister on her wedding day.

Aunt Myrtle had established herself in the dining room, where an array of snacks covered the table. Keeping a prudent distance between himself and that cane was a lifelong habit.

He leaned against the sink. *Mom could use a small television in here.* A peal of laughter rang through the house. *Not that I could hear it over the ruckus those girls were making.*

Mom stepped into the room carrying an empty bowl. "There you are, Derrick. Could you hand me the rest of the pretzels? They're in the cabinet behind you."

"Sure." He took down the half-full bag and emptied it into the bowl she held.

"Thanks, honey." She started to leave.

"Anything else you need me to do?"

She turned a half smile on him. "You're bored, aren't you?"

"Of course not. Why would you say that?"

Mom arched her brows and looked at him over the top of her glasses. He grinned. Mom always knew when he was lying.

"Well, there doesn't seem to be much for me to do here," he admitted. "Are there any errands Chelsea needs me to run? Any last-minute things to pick up?"

Mom shook her head. "We've got everything under control. Aunt Myrtle even finished all the birdseed favors." Her face assumed a fake guileless expression. "Maybe the musicians need some help getting their instruments over to the church."

Aunt Myrtle has a big mouth.

Derrick let out a groan, and Mom laughed. She set the pretzel bowl on the table and folded her arms. "So tell me about this violin player. She seemed like a nice girl, from what I saw at the rehearsal last night."

Derrick leaned an elbow on the counter. "She's independent, that's for sure. An only child. Smart. Classy. A city girl, not crazy about sports. And she loves music. Playing it, I mean."

"For someone you just met yesterday, you seem to know a lot about her."

Derrick lifted a shoulder. "Well, I read her profile page on ShoutLife before she got here." He glanced away. "And, uh, I did show her around the festival a little this afternoon. We talked."

Interest brightened Mom's eyes. "Really?"

From the other room, Chelsea's voice called, "Mom, where are you? I want you to look at this shade of blush."

Mom glanced toward the door. "Coming, honey," she called, then lowered her voice to speak to Derrick. "I want to hear more about this girl later." She picked up the pretzels. "Oh, and Derrick, you don't have to hang around here."

Derrick glanced toward the door. "But what if Chelsea needs me?"

Mom smiled. "She won't even notice you're gone." The smile faded into a stern look. "Just don't be late for the wedding."

She left the room. Feeling as though he'd been let out of prison, Derrick fished his keys out of his pocket. If he hurried, he could get to the hotel in time to see Jazzy judge at least part of the pageant.

The talent competition was worse, if possible, than the poise-and-stage-presence portion of the pageant. At least on the judges.

Jazzy sat rigidly upright in her chair, her face aching from holding a painted-on smile since the beginning of this torturous ordeal. Seemed every kid in Waynesboro cherished aspirations of singing in a country-and-western band. Didn't anybody want to play an instrument anymore?

What time was it, anyway? She hated to glance at her watch

again. Everyone in the audience would know how impatient she was for this stupid pageant to end. Besides, she was acutely aware that her every move was being noted and commented upon in hushed whispers throughout the room.

The current contestant—Jazzy couldn't remember her name, but her number was fourteen—finished a rendition of "Paper Roses" that would have made Marie Osmond run screaming from the room. Jazzy clamped her jaws against a powerful yawn and recorded her score on the sheet in front of her.

"And next, we have contestant number fifteen, Miss Heidi Baldwin," announced Kate. "Heidi will entertain us with her baton-twirling skills. Heidi, whenever you're ready."

Jazzy clasped her hands together in her lap. Poor Heidi stepped to the center of the stage holding a baton at each side. Her hands trembled so violently that the metallic pom-poms on the ends of her batons shimmered in the harsh spotlight. Was it Jazzy's imagination, or had the air suddenly become heavy with tension? Nearly palpable waves of nervous sympathy wafted from the audience toward the obviously miserable girl.

Speakers mounted on poles at each corner of the stage crackled to life, pouring forth the strains of "Stars and Stripes Forever." For one queasy moment Jazzy thought Heidi wasn't going to snap out of her panic-induced coma, but then her hours of rehearsal kicked in. The girl's face cleared and she launched into action. With a relieved sigh, Jazzy leaned back in her chair and watched Heidi march around the stage, twirling her batons in mesmerizing patterns. They glittered as they spun and twisted with intricate precision, and only once did one fall to the stage. But that was after a high launch in the air, and moments later Heidi repeated the move and caught it flawlessly. She ended with a complicated flourish and a triumphant drop to one knee.

Jazzy joined in the applause as the girl marched off the stage with a relieved smile. But when she tallied the score, Jazzy's heart grew heavy in her chest. Heidi's total fell far short of most of the other girls'. There was no possible way she could walk away with the Little Princess crown today.

As she shuffled her score sheets into a neat stack, a movement in the audience snagged Jazzy's attention. A cautious glance showed her that Irene had left her chair and was heading toward the rear of the ballroom. Her towering figure disappeared into the darkness that lay beyond the reach of the bright stage lights. Apparently the woman didn't want to wait around to see the rest of the competitors. But at least that meant Jazzy would no longer be subjected to the weight of her menacing stare.

Feeling lighter than she had all afternoon, Jazzy turned her attention to contestant number sixteen.

Jazzy paced the confines of the curtained-off area that had been set aside for the judges in the corner of the International Ballroom. Noise from the restless crowd beyond the fabric barrier rose in volume with each passing minute as the families of the competitors waited for the crowning of this year's Little Princess. Tan Woman sat at a card table doing the final tabulation of their combined scores with the calculator from Jazzy's planner, while Kate and her sister sat watching.

Jazzy glanced at her watch for the fifth time. "I have *got* to get out of here. You don't keep a bride waiting on her wedding day."

Kate looked calmly at the watch on her own pudgy wrist. "It will take you ten minutes to get to the church. It's only five after right now. Didn't you say you're supposed to start playing at five-thirty?"

Jazzy spoke through clenched teeth. "We have to load our instruments into the car, and when we get there it'll take some time to set up and tune."

"Done!" Tan Woman raised a triumphant grin. "You want to check it over?"

She held the page toward Jazzy. Though her brain kept urging *Hurry! Hurry! Hurry!*, Jazzy forced herself to take the sheet and glance over the numbers. A couple of quick mental calculations matched Tan Woman's totals exactly. No surprises in the results, either. The winner enjoyed a twelve-point lead over the first runner-up. Jazzy noted Heidi Baldwin's total fell solidly in the middle of the group. Better than she'd expected, actually.

"Looks good to me." She thrust the paper toward Kate. "Can I go now?"

Kate heaved herself out of the chair. "I want to thank you again for helping us out," she said as she pumped Jazzy's hand. "I really appreciate it."

Jazzy started to say, "Glad to do it," but that would be a total lie. Instead she flashed a smile at all three women as she snatched up her sweater and hurried through the curtain.

When she stepped into view on the other side, a hush fell over the audience. A hundred expectant faces turned toward her. For one moment, Jazzy's head swam as panic dimmed the edges of her vision.

They were all staring at her.

Someone took her arm, and a comforting voice spoke close enough that soft breath tickled her ear. "Are you ready to blow this place?"

Slow warmth crept over her as she looked up into Derrick's face. Her heart sprang with a giddy leap into her throat. Why had she not noticed that his eyes were exactly the same shade as the hot cocoa her grandma used to fix for her on snowy winter nights? A girl could get lost in dreamy eyes like those.

Her face hot, she recovered herself as he guided her toward

the exit with a gentle pressure on her arm. "What are you doing here? Where are Liz and Caitlin?" she asked.

"Waiting out front in my truck. They left with Matt about ten minutes ago to load up your instruments and Old Sue so we could skedaddle as soon as you were finished."

"Okay, so why are you here instead of at the church with your sister?"

"I figured I'd stop by and get my dog." A smile played around the corners of his mouth. "And offer you a ride to the church."

Pulse fluttering, Jazzy glanced at his clothing. "Surely you're not planning to walk your sister down the aisle in jeans?"

"My tux is waiting for me in the groom's room." A crooked grin replaced the half smile. "It doesn't take a guy hours to get dressed, you know. Unlike some women I could name."

As they neared the exit, Jazzy risked a last glance toward the watching crowd. Like a magnet to metal, her gaze was drawn to the one she would have given anything to avoid. Irene's dagger-like stare sliced across the fifty feet that separated them. What would Irene do when she found out Heidi didn't win, didn't even place as a runner-up? Jazzy steeled her nerves and her expression. A second later she was through the door and, thankfully, out of sight.

NINETEEN

As Derrick led Jazzy past the front desk, Emmy leaned over the counter to flag them down.

"Oh, Miss Delaney, there you are." Emmy's face was drawn with worry as she hurried through the half door to intercept them.

With a quick glance toward the front doors, Derrick's jaw tightened as he stopped. He checked his watch. They had fifteen minutes to get to the church, and the girls still had to get their instruments out and set up and do whatever else musicians did before they started playing.

"We're in kind of a hurry," he told Emmy. "Did you need something?"

Her hands clasped and unclasped in front of her waist, those ridiculous fingernails flashing with every move. "I tried to call Miss Delaney's room about half an hour ago, but I couldn't get an answer." She clamped down on her lower lip nervously. "I wanted to talk to one of those sheriff deputies who've been hanging around back there all day."

Derrick frowned. "Why do you need a deputy? Is something wrong?"

"I think so. It's Mr. Goggins. We can't find him anywhere. Nobody's seen him for hours. I'm afraid something might have happened to him."

Jazzy laid a comforting hand on the girl's arm. "I'm sure he's fine. He probably had an errand to run, something to do with the festival."

Emmy shook her head. "That's just it. This is one of the hotel's busiest days of the whole year. Mr. Goggins wouldn't disappear on festival weekend. He should be right here, helping out and making sure everything goes smoothly."

"When was the last time you saw him?" Jazzy's tone was unrushed, but she telegraphed her urgency in the tense muscles of the arm Derrick still held. He was starting to share her anxiety about getting to the church on time.

"A little after two. A customer demanded to see him, complaining about the lighting in her bathroom. He took care of that, and he went back into his office. Said something about checking up on somebody. That was the last time we saw him."

Derrick exchanged a glance with Jazzy. That was shortly after they'd left Bradley's office three hours ago.

"I'm sure he's fine," Derrick told the obviously distraught girl. "But I'm going to see the sheriff in about ten minutes. I'll mention your concerns. If he thinks there's anything wrong, I'm sure he'll send someone over to talk to you. Okay?"

Emmy did not look convinced, but she nodded and let them go.

As Derrick steered Jazzy through the front doors toward his pickup parked beneath the entryway awning, she lifted worried eyes toward him. "I hope Bradley is okay."

"He's fine. Knowing him, he probably slipped off to a corner somewhere to hide until the rush is over."

Actually, Derrick didn't feel as confident as he tried to sound. He had a sneaking suspicion the teenager was right, and Bradley might be headed for trouble. But whether the man was in trouble or causing trouble, Derrick couldn't guess.

* * *

"Sorry I'm late." Jazzy slipped into the front seat of Derrick's pickup and sent an apologetic grimace toward the back.

Liz scowled. "Took you long enough. We were trying to figure out if we could do the wedding march as a cello-flute duet. And counting our money, because we were planning to split your share."

"Stop it!" Caitlin slapped at Liz's leg. "We were not." She looked up at Jazzy. "Who won?"

On the other side of the rear window, Old Sue stood in the truck bed and stared mournfully into the cab. Her wet nose smeared yucky-looking tracks across the glass. Jazzy resisted the urge to jump out and wipe the window clean. Instead she answered Caitlin's question. "Number eight."

"Is she the one who sang the Shania Twain song?"

Jazzy shook her head. "No, that was twelve, and she came in second. Number eight tap-danced to 'Boot Scootin' Boogie.'"

"Oh, yeah." Caitlin settled back in the seat with a smile. "I liked her outfit. Those white cowgirl boots were adorable."

Liz rolled her eyes as the driver's door opened and Derrick climbed in. "Matt and Frank are going to give us an escort." He gripped the top of the wheel with both hands and flashed a maniacal grin at Jazzy. "I've always wanted to go blasting through red lights at sixty miles an hour."

Jazzy shoved the seat belt into the clasp until she heard the click. "Hold on, Old Sue," she shouted out the window. "Speed Racer is at the wheel."

Actually, the drive to the church was frustratingly slow even with a police escort. Many of Waynesboro's downtown streets had been rerouted to handle the festival crowd, and no amount of flashing lights or sirens could push the slow-moving traffic to a faster pace. Jazzy's stomach muscles grew tighter with every minute that ticked by.

Finally they pulled into the church parking lot. Derrick zoomed around the building and parked his truck in a no-parking zone right next to the back steps. Old Sue watched as they grabbed their instruments from the back, her legs trembling expectantly.

"Come on, girl," Derrick told the dog. "You'll be more comfortable waiting in the cab."

Old Sue leaped down from the bed and then jumped obediently into the front seat at Derrick's command.

"Will she be okay?" Jazzy asked as they dashed toward the door.

"She'll be fine." Derrick lunged ahead to open the door and hold it for them. "The windows are down, and the evening isn't too hot. Besides, she'd much rather snooze on a soft seat than in that hard truck bed."

As they sprinted through a maze of Sunday-school rooms toward the sanctuary, Jazzy realized she had left her sweater in the truck.

Terrific. It'll be covered in dog hair.

At five-forty, ten minutes late, Caitlin gave the count for their first piece. Jazzy's toes picked up the pace and on the downbeat she launched into the first chord of the Handel aria. The church pews in front of her were filling rapidly as tuxedo-clad groomsmen ushered a steady stream of people to empty seats. More faces turned her way here than back at the pageant, and for a moment her vision wavered. The familiar panic threatened to paralyze her bow arm. She closed her eyes.

Focus on your real audience, Jazzy. Music is your gift to God. Give Him your best.

That's how she had overcome the worst of her stage fright, by learning to block out the watching eyes and focus instead on creating a beautiful offering to the One who had given her the gift of music. As she drew the bow across the strings of her instrument, her body swayed back and forth in time with the soothing melody. Everything else in the room faded into an untroubling blur.

At the conclusion of their fourth song she felt a nudge against her foot. Jazzy opened her eyes to see Caitlin watching the door at the back of the sanctuary. The wedding coordinator stood at attention, and when she caught their eyes, she gave a nod for the processional to begin.

Jazzy couldn't close her eyes during this number, because she needed to watch for the bridal march cue. As the groom and pastor filed through a side door and took their places before the altar, Jazzy risked a glance into the sanctuary. A familiar face caught her eye. Sheriff Maguire looked completely different in a tuxedo than he did in his uniform. More dignified. Stately, even. Seated next to him was an attractive woman who must be the groom's mother.

Jazzy wondered if Derrick had remembered to mention Bradley to Sheriff Maguire. Probably not. He'd barely had enough time to get into his tux and dash to the bride room.

Curious, Jazzy glanced across the aisle. What did Derrick's mother look like? She hadn't paid much attention during the rehearsal yesterday. But she could have picked this lady out in a crowd. Both her son and her daughter looked remarkably like her. Blond hair, trim build, a kind expression that just now wore the tearful smile of one whose pride in her offspring was overwhelming. Beside her perched the sturdy frame of Derrick's aunt Myrtle, both hands planted squarely on the top of her cane. Aunt Myrtle caught Jazzy's eye and gave her a complimentary thumbs-up. Jazzy smiled in response.

While the flower girl spread her trail of bright-red petals on the silky aisle runner, the doors at the back of the sanctuary closed. The little girl took her place at the front of the line of bridesmaids. Jazzy, Liz and Caitlin finished the piece. An expectant hush fell over the wedding guests. At just the right moment, Caitlin bobbed her head. With practiced timing, they launched into the familiar strains of the bridal march.

The doors opened. Everyone stood and turned in their pews, necks straining to see the bride. A collective "Ah!" rose from those gathered at the sight of Chelsea, resplendent in a classic A-line design of white lace. Jazzy had played for dozens of weddings, and she never tired of the emotional response that filled the sanctuary when the guests got their first glimpse of the bride.

But today Jazzy had a hard time focusing on the bride. Hummingbirds fluttered behind her breastbone at the sight of the incredibly handsome man on Chelsea's arm. For a guy who preferred to spend his time tromping through dirty woods or skewering worms with fishhooks, Derrick Rogers sure did look at home in a tux. A question formed in her mind and transformed itself into a prayer.

Lord, is he the one for me?

She tore her gaze away and focused on the music, on the proper positioning of her bow, on the smooth motion of drawing it across the violin's strings. Anything but the chocolate-eyed tuxedo-clad heartthrob making his way down the aisle, drawing nearer with every step.

When the bride took her place, the ceremony began. Jazzy didn't hear a word. She focused all her energy on trying not to get locked into Derrick's gaze. Her skin burned from the red-hot touch of his eyes as he stared at her.

The door at the back of the sanctuary cracked open.

The flutter in her chest became a heavy thud. A uniformed deputy stepped into view. Even across the length of the sanctuary, Jazzy could see by the man's expression that something terrible had happened.

TWENTY

The deputy's head swiveled as he scanned the sanctuary. Jazzy didn't recognize him. Thank goodness the wedding party had turned to face the altar. The minister—the only person looking in that direction besides the musicians—continued with his ceremony without missing a beat. Chelsea stared with bridal rapture at her groom, oblivious to anything happening around her. Jazzy doubted if she even heard the minister's words, much less the quiet murmur of the guests seated in the last couple of pews who had turned their heads to gawk at the interruption.

When the deputy caught sight of Sheriff Maguire, he started down the aisle. The wedding coordinator stepped into view, her expression fierce. She grabbed his arm and pulled him off the silken aisle runner. Chastened, the man obediently hurried around the side of the sanctuary.

No doubt where he was headed. Jazzy tracked his progress to the second pew, where he sidestepped across the wedding guests until he reached the sheriff. He touched the sheriff's tuxedo-clad shoulder and whispered in his ear.

The minister's voice cut into the quiet drama with increased volume. "Who gives this woman to be married to this man?"

Jazzy's attention snapped back to the ceremony. This was Derrick's big moment.

The tender gaze he turned on his sister twisted Jazzy's heart in her chest. His voice rang throughout the sanctuary. "Her family, who loves her."

He bestowed a gentle kiss on her cheek, and then placed her hand in Quinn's. Tears sparkled in Chelsea's eyes as she tore her gaze away from her groom to smile up at her brother.

As Derrick stepped backward to sit beside his mother and Aunt Myrtle, he caught sight of the deputy whispering in the sheriff's ear. For the space of a few seconds, Derrick froze, before he slid into his seat.

Jazzy exchanged a glance with Liz, who lifted her shoulders with a slow gesture. Whatever had happened must be pretty important. Jazzy couldn't imagine how anyone would have the nerve to interrupt Sheriff Maguire at his son's wedding. With a sick quiver in her stomach, she realized it must have something to do with the murder case. Had they found another victim? *Lord, please no!*

The sheriff apparently considered the interruption justified. With a quick glance at his wife, whose glare could have ignited wet wood, he slipped out of the pew. He tromped down the center aisle, oblivious to the havoc his shiny black shoes wreaked on the trail of rose petals. At least the deputy was careful to follow along the edge of the silken runner.

Jazzy saw Derrick's head turn as he watched the duo's progress. When he faced forward again, his gaze sought hers.

Her fear was reflected in his eyes.

Whispers spread among the wedding-reception guests like flames on a dried-up Christmas tree.

"Any idea what's going on?"

"Why do you think the sheriff left in the *middle* of the ceremony?"

"Did you see the look on Maddie Maguire's face? I don't envy the sheriff when she gets him alone."

Derrick smiled and gave a noncommittal nod as he threaded through the crowd balancing three plastic punch cups. The church's fellowship hall had been transformed to host Chelsea's reception. Delicious odors wafted from a line of silver chafing dishes that would provide a buffet dinner for the guests when the photographer finished with the wedding party. Derrick wove between glitter-covered tables and twisted sideways in time to miss a couple of kids dashing across the otherwise empty dance floor in pursuit of a shiny white balloon.

"It's outrageous, that's what it is." He approached the corner where the musicians were setting up their music stands in time to hear Aunt Myrtle's pronouncement on the interruption. "What kind of family has Chelsea married into? I can't imagine anything so important it couldn't wait half an hour for the ceremony to end."

"Sheriff Maguire is a public servant, Aunt Myrtle." Derrick extended his cup-laden hands toward Jazzy. "And he's in the middle of the murder investigation."

Jazzy set a piece of music on the metal stand in front of her before relieving him of one of the brimming cups. A single line creased the smooth skin between her wide eyes. "You don't think there's been another victim, do you?"

"I sure hope not," Liz said as she took the punch he held toward her.

Flute resting across her lap, Caitlin remained silent. She set her cup untouched on the floor beneath her chair.

"At least he came back before the end of the ceremony," Jazzy said. "He got to hear them say their vows."

"Which proves my point." Aunt Myrtle's hard lips drew up

like she'd bitten a crab apple. "That officer obviously could have waited a few minutes. There was no need to destroy Chelsea's wedding, after her poor mother's effort to make it perfect."

Derrick was about to protest that the wedding had certainly not been ruined when Jazzy said smoothly, "It was a beautiful wedding. We've played at a good number of them, and this was one of the nicest. Don't you think so, girls?"

"Absolutely," Caitlin answered.

"Oh yes, one of the nicest for sure." Liz's reply as she shuffled through a stack of papers on her stand sounded a little rehearsed, but Aunt Myrtle didn't seem to notice.

"You girls played beautifully." The old woman placed heavily-ringed fingers to her collarbone and closed her eyes in an ecstasy of appreciation. "I've never heard Handel played with such feeling, such artistry. You know," she lowered her voice and dipped her head, "I was an accomplished pianist in my day."

Derrick bit back a blast of laughter before it escaped his lips. He remembered agonizing hours of being forced to sit on the scratchy cloth sofa while Aunt Myrtle gave one of her concerts. Even as a boy without a trace of musical ability, he'd recognized bad playing. He caught Jazzy's glance and winked. An answering blush colored her cheeks.

"If only someone had inherited my talent. But Derrick and Chelsea were both born with tin ears." Aunt Myrtle cast a withering glance his way, then turned a beseeching smile on Jazzy. "Perhaps if Derrick marries wisely, there's hope for the next generation of Rogers children."

Derrick failed to stop an embarrassed groan. Leave it to Aunt Myrtle. Jazzy's blush deepened to fiery red. Caitlin and Liz both became busy with their instruments, though Derrick glimpsed their amused grins.

A commotion behind him provided a welcome interruption.

He turned in time to see the bride and groom step through the doorway arm in arm, followed by the bridal party.

"The photographer is finished. Finally!" Aunt Myrtle waved an impatient hand in Derrick's direction. "Derrick Stephen, escort me to my seat."

With Aunt Myrtle leaning heavily on his arm, Derrick cast one last apologetic glance toward Jazzy as he made his way across the dance floor toward the head table.

"What took so long?" Aunt Myrtle demanded of Chelsea as she dropped into the chair Derrick slid out for her. "I took my pill twenty minutes ago, and you know the doctor says I must eat within thirty minutes."

Derrick didn't wait around to hear Chelsea's answer. He spotted Sheriff Maguire on the other side of the room, his expression grim. The sheriff bent slightly at the waist as Mrs. Maguire whispered rather intently into his ear. When he caught sight of Derrick's approach, his eyes lit and he straightened.

"Good to see you, son." The man greeted Derrick with so much enthusiasm no one would have guessed they'd just seen each other a few hours before. "Looks like we're officially relatives now."

When Derrick clasped his hand the sheriff pulled him away from Mrs. Maguire, whose stern expression clearly indicated her determination to continue their interrupted conversation at the earliest opportunity. Derrick flashed an apologetic smile toward the woman and allowed himself to be hauled into a corner. Only when their escape was secure did the sheriff release him.

He pulled a handkerchief out of his pocket and mopped at his sweaty brow. "I'd rather face the criminal element than that woman when she's got a burr under her saddle."

Derrick chose the wise man's course and didn't reply to that comment. "I haven't had a chance to see you since we got here.

When I left the hotel the girl at the front desk asked me to let you know that Goggins hasn't been seen all afternoon. She seemed pretty worried."

The sheriff shot him a quick glance through narrowed lids, but his only reply was a single nod.

Derrick studied the closed expression. "That deputy must have had something important to tell you."

Sheriff Maguire shoved the handkerchief back in his pocket. "You might say that."

"An important discovery? A new clue, maybe?"

The man didn't answer.

"Not another body, I hope."

"Nope."

The sheriff stared across the room, where Chelsea and Quinn were accepting the best wishes of their guests. At that moment Jazzy and her friends launched into a stately tune, which lent an elegant atmosphere to the decorated church basement. Derrick studied his sister's new father-in-law, who refused to meet his gaze.

"You're not going to tell me, are you?"

"Nope."

"I just thought since we're sort of relatives now—"

Sheriff Maguire cut him off with a glance. Apparently "sort of relatives" didn't warrant inside police information.

"Well, I hope whatever it was means Jazzy and her friends are finally safe."

The sheriff's gaze slid sideways to lock on to Derrick's. His lips formed a grim line.

A lump of icy dread trickled down Derrick's throat and landed deep in his core. "You mean they're in danger?"

Maguire spoke so quietly Derrick almost didn't catch his words. "Let's just say I'm not canceling their guard yet."

TWENTY-ONE

The wedding guests applauded politely while the trio gracefully finished their last number. Jazzy placed her violin in its plush velvet-lined case and closed the lid.

As Caitlin twisted the pieces of her flute apart she grinned at Jazzy. "That was one of our better performances, I think."

Liz, stooping over her cello case, agreed. "The bride seems pleased, anyway."

Jazzy glanced at the head table, where Chelsea clapped with enthusiasm. Her gaze then intersected Derrick's, two seats away from his sister. The intensity in his eyes as he applauded made Jazzy duck her head, her cheeks burning. "Well, we earned our fee tonight."

"Trust me," Liz said, straightening, "we have more than earned our fee with this gig."

Given all they'd been through, Jazzy had to agree.

The disc jockey, a spiky-haired kid with an impressive soundboard, picked up a microphone and stepped out into the middle of the dance floor. "Ladies and gentlemen, let's hear it for the old-lady music—I mean the *classical* ensemble."

The kid turned an impish grin their way, and Jazzy stuck a playful tongue out in his direction, which made the crowd laugh.

"But now that you've filled your bellies, are you ready to get down and boogie?" The kid was in possession of an obvious ham bone, perfect for a live DJ. The crowd answered with a smattering of applause. "Yeah, yeah, you'll get your turn. But first, Chelsea and Quinn are going to inaugurate this dance floor with the traditional first dance."

Music blared from giant black speakers as the bride and groom moved to the center of the dance floor. Jazzy picked up her sheet music and placed it in her leather portfolio. As she fastened the clasps, she stole a glance at the newlyweds. A sentimental wave threatened to flood her eyes when she glimpsed the love shining on Quinn's face as he stared down at his bride.

A respectful few minutes into the song, more couples made their way onto the dance floor.

"Surprise, surprise," mumbled Liz. "Look who's heading this way."

Jazzy turned in the direction she indicated, and found herself face-to-face with Derrick.

"Would you do me the honor?" The warmth in his eyes sent a flush to her cheeks.

Jazzy stared at the hand he extended. She could name about a dozen reasons why she shouldn't step onto a dance floor with this guy. Their lack of common interests topped the list. But no matter how many reasons she could come up with *not* to get involved with Derrick Rogers, one fact remained: his were the dreamiest eyes she'd ever had the opportunity to gaze into.

Caitlin placed a hand on her back. "Go ahead. We'll get everything else packed up and then grab something to eat."

Jazzy felt herself shoved gently forward, right into Derrick's waiting arms. He whisked her to the center of the dance floor before she could protest.

For a few awkward moments their feet bumped into each other and Jazzy fought to keep her hand from clenching his tuxedo-clad shoulder. Her gaze searched the room—anywhere but his face—and she caught a glimpse of Aunt Myrtle's triumphant gleam and Chelsea's encouraging nod. Then they settled into a rhythm as Jazzy matched his movements in reverse. For a guy who spent a lot of time sending worms to their watery graves, Derrick sure seemed comfortable on a dance floor.

The silence that stretched between them was starting to feel strained. "Uh, I saw you talking with the sheriff earlier. Did he tell you what that deputy said?"

For an instant Derrick's hand tightened on hers, but then he relaxed. "He wouldn't say much. Just that they haven't discovered another victim."

Jazzy searched his face. His eyes did not meet hers. Was he holding something back? "It must not have been too important, or I guess he would have had to leave, huh?"

He lifted the shoulder her hand rested on. "I guess. But he did say he was keeping a guard assigned to you and Liz and Caitlin." He looked down at her then, a frown hovering at the corners of his eyes. "Just stick close to them tonight, okay?"

Jazzy fought the temptation to become irritated with his protective advice. She was a grown woman, and she didn't need him to tell her to stick close to her friends. But she also knew he was right. All she had to do was close her eyes to hear Liz's scream as it pierced the night. She shuddered. "Don't worry. I'm not going anywhere except right back to the hotel room tonight."

"I hope you'll stay here for a while. This DJ is pretty good, and we've got him booked 'til midnight."

Jazzy shook her head. "Sitting in a chair and playing an instrument for a couple of hours might not look like hard work, but honestly, after a performance like this we're pretty wiped out. We'll just have something to eat and then head back to the hotel."

If she had her preference, she'd skip the buffet here in favor of room service. Let Bradley buy her dinner tonight. She suddenly remembered Emmy's concern. "I hope nothing's happened to Bradley."

Derrick's mouth tightened. "If he has disappeared, it might mean I was right."

"Or wrong," Jazzy said. No matter how incriminating the circumstances, she just couldn't see the friendly hotel manager murdering someone.

Derrick changed the subject. "What time are you leaving tomorrow?"

"Right after Caitlin and Liz are finished judging. Probably around two." Worry gnawed in her belly, and she blurted out the question that had plagued her since Liz was attacked. "You don't think the killer will follow us home, do you?"

Derrick's hand tightened on her waist. His expression was grim. "Let's pray they catch the guy before you leave, and then we won't have to worry about that."

Jazzy noticed he didn't answer her question. The worry transformed into a knot of fear.

"Okay, I think that's it."

Jazzy stepped back from Matt's cruiser as he slammed the trunk, their instruments stowed inside. Derrick walked her around to the passenger side of the vehicle while Matt circled to the driver's door. Liz and Caitlin were already in the backseat.

Derrick reached for the door handle, then paused. "Wait a minute."

He went to his truck and leaned through the open window. Old Sue, who'd been freed from the front seat by a pack of the younger wedding guests, ran across the church lawn toward him with a ball in her mouth. Jazzy's lips tightened when she saw Old Sue drop the ball, plant her feet on Derrick's chest and greet him with a tongue on the cheek. She might be willing to admit that Old Sue was a pretty cool animal, but there was no telling how many germs resided in dog slobber. One of the kids snatched the ball and took off, Old Sue in hot pursuit, apparently having the time of her life.

The sun had disappeared from view in the sky behind Derrick. Jazzy squinted to see his face in the deepening twilight when he trotted back toward her. "Listen, I've been thinking about you not having a cell phone for a while, so I want you to take this." He thrust a phone into her hand.

"Derrick, I can't take yours. I'll get another one." She tried to give it back to him, but he hid his hands behind his back.

"That'll take time, and you need a phone. Besides, I have an ulterior motive." His grin held enough mischievous charm to make her pulse flutter. "When the sheriff is finished with yours, I intend to drive to Lexington and trade."

A rush of pleasure weakened her knees. She couldn't look him in the eye as she dropped the phone into the deep pockets of her loose slacks. "Will we see you tomorrow?" she managed to stammer.

"You bet." He ducked his head, forcing her to look up. "Want to have breakfast? Say around eight?"

Struggling to swallow a ridiculous giggle, Jazzy didn't trust herself to speak. She nodded.

He opened the door for her to slide in. Matt fired up the engine as she snapped her seat belt in place, her eyes glued to the window. Derrick didn't move, but stood watching as the cruiser pulled out of the church parking lot. Jazzy kept him in her sights until the car turned onto the street and he was lost to view.

She turned in her seat to speak to Liz and Caitlin, only to find them staring at her, knowing smirks plastered across their faces.

Liz shook her head. "Girl, you have got it *bad.*"

* * *

The nice thing about riding with a deputy was that they didn't have to worry about finding a parking spot in the hotel's overflowing lot. Matt parked the cruiser on the yellow line next to the front entrance. Jazzy got out and waited for him to pop the trunk. From somewhere in the distance, live bluegrass music drifted to her ears, carried on a warm breeze.

The car door slammed behind Caitlin. "Wow. Would you look at that crowd?"

Jazzy followed her gaze, eyes wide with amazement. The sheer number of people who packed the festival route was impressive, and a little intimidating. All traces of sunlight had now disappeared for the night, and a bright half-moon stood sentinel over the festivities. Floodlights positioned on both sides of the street warded off the darkness. A dozen columns of smoke rose toward the inky, purplish sky from barbecue pits that had burned for more than a day. The pungent odors of burning wood and roasting meat saturated the deep breath Jazzy drew into her lungs.

Liz closed her eyes, nose high in the air. "Mmmmm. The baked chicken at the wedding was good, but something over there is calling my name."

Jazzy nudged her ribs with a laugh. "Tomorrow you'll get to try every bit of barbecue the festival has to offer. We might even convince you to taste burgoo."

A delicate shudder shook Liz's frame. "Don't hold your breath."

They hefted their instrument cases out of the trunk and into the hotel. The bluegrass music ended abruptly when the doors closed behind them. Jazzy thought she wouldn't mind checking out a few of the bands booked to play at the festival tomorrow. She had torn a concert schedule out of the paper she'd picked up yesterday and tucked it into the side pocket of her—

"Oh, rats!" She came to a halt. Matt, Caitlin and Liz turned questioning glances her way. "I left my planner in the judge's room after the pageant. Hang on a second."

She veered toward the front desk. Maybe Kate had dropped it off there for her to pick up. And besides, she wanted to ask if there was any word from Bradley.

Jazzy approached the matronly woman behind the desk. Emmy must have left for the day. "Did someone turn in a black leather planner? I left it in the ballroom after the Little Princess pageant."

The woman opened a deep drawer and peered inside. "No, honey, I'm sorry. Maybe it's still in there, though."

"Okay, thanks. One more question. Has Mr. Goggins come back?"

Sudden worry deepened the creases in her pleasant face. "I'm sorry, but Mr. Goggins isn't here."

"Has he not been here all evening?"

Jazzy thought the woman was getting ready to say something, but she shook her head. "Is there something I can do for you?"

"No, that's okay."

She rejoined Matt and the girls, who stood waiting beside the threadbare sofa. "Bradley's still missing in action." She placed her violin on the cushion. "Listen, I'm going to run in there and grab my planner. Wait here for me, okay?"

The deputy shook his head. "No, ma'am. I have strict orders to escort you back to your room."

"But it's just inside the ballroom, right down that hallway."

A stubborn set took hold of his jaw. "The sheriff told me to see you back to your room."

Irritation surged through her. "Honestly, Matt. I'm going to run around that corner," she said, pointing to the hallway just past the front desk, "slip into the ballroom and get my planner from behind that little curtained-off area. I won't be in there ninety seconds."

"Then we'll go with you."

Jazzy fought down the urge to stomp her foot. There were people scattered all over the lobby. Nothing could happen in such a public place. Police protection was one thing. Police *over*-protection bordered on the ridiculous. "Liz is carrying a cello, for crying out loud. Besides looking like a marching band, we'll disrupt the Miss Bar-B-Q Pageant if we all tromp into the room. Just wait here. I'll be right back."

She didn't give him a chance to argue further, but jogged away in the direction of the ballroom.

A few people loitered outside the door to the International Ballroom. At the far end of the hallway, big, metal double doors had been thrown open to the outside, and the smoky smell of the festival barbecue pits invaded the corridor. A small group huddled near the door leading into the ballroom, and one lady leaned sideways to press her ear to the crack. She straightened and turned to those gathered around her. "They're taking a break so the judges can tally their scores and select the finalists."

Good. Jazzy could slip inside during the break, grab her planner and get out without drawing attention to herself.

The door was thrown wide, and a large crowd of people filed through. Most headed outside through the far doors, though a few wandered in the direction of the lobby. Jazzy backed up against the wall and waited for the crowd to thin.

The top of an auburn head bobbing her way grabbed her attention. Someone was coming toward her, pushing upstream through the crowd in the opposite direction.

A break opened in the sea of bodies, and Jazzy looked directly into the face of the one person she'd hoped she would never lay eyes on again.

Irene Baldwin.

The menace in the woman's glare sent fear streaking down Jazzy's spine.

Instinct took over. She whirled and ran.

TWENTY-TWO

The song ended, and Derrick released his mother's hand to applaud. She looked so nice in her mother-of-the-bride dress. The peachy flush that flirted with her cheeks erased the strain that had begun to hang heavily on her in recent weeks. He realized with a start that she was still a young woman, not yet fifty. A lot of years stretched before her, years that could be spent in the company of a second husband if she so desired.

He brushed that idea away. Weddings were dangerous. They wreaked havoc on a guy's thoughts. Like earlier on the dance floor, when he'd held Jazzy in his arms.

Thoughts of Jazzy made him smile. She had really opened up today at the festival. No doubt Old Sue had made an impression on her. And this evening after the pageant, when she'd looked into his eyes…the same way Chelsea was looking at Quinn right now.

He gave himself a mental shake. Yep. Weddings were dangerous.

"Is it warm in here, or is it just me?" Mom fanned her face with a hand.

"It's not you." Derrick and the other guys in the penguin suits had lost their ties and jackets a while ago.

The next song started, this one a little too fast for Derrick's comfort level. He was relieved when Mom said, "I think I'll sit this one out."

He guided her toward her seat. When they rounded the edge of the table, she stumbled when her foot scuffed over the thick black cable running from the DJ's soundboard to a speaker in a corner. Derrick supported her with a firm grip on her arm.

"Oh, my!" Mom frowned at the cord. "Someone's going to trip over that and hurt themselves."

Derrick agreed. "The other one is out of the way, but he should have taped this one down. I think I'll grab some masking tape."

He saw her to her seat and then slipped out of the fellowship hall. The church's storage area, where they kept extra chairs and tables as well as a variety of supplies, was down a short hallway. Derrick let himself into the room and flipped on the light.

Let's see, where would they keep masking tape? He rummaged through the junk piled on a set of deep metal shelves along one wall. A box of miscellaneous electrical equipment. A couple of old, banged-up collection plates. Several pairs of glittery angel wings from the annual Christmas pageant. But no masking tape. Maybe he'd find a roll in one of the kitchen drawers.

As he turned to leave, Derrick noticed a bundle in the far corner. It rested on the floor beneath a dozen or so shepherd crooks. An army-green duffel bag. Not unusual in itself, but what snagged his attention was something dangling down the side. It looked like hair.

Stooping on his haunches, Derrick grabbed a canvas handle and pulled the bag toward him. It was hair, a long ponytail of gray hair attached to the back of a baseball cap. Stupid-looking thing, obviously a gag of some sort. He wouldn't be caught dead wearing something like that. Now where had he heard something about a gray ponytail lately?

He pulled the cap out of the bag, and when he did a tri-fold brochure fluttered to the floor.

When he looked down at the paper, shock coursed through his body.

He was staring at Jazzy's face.

TWENTY-THREE

Alarms rang in her head. Jazzy knew she should double back, head for the hotel lobby and the safety of Matt's presence. But Irene was behind her. The back of her skull tingled with the certainty that those eyes were fixed on her. She couldn't make herself turn around. Instead, she huddled in the center of the pageant crowd and allowed herself to be swept through the hotel's exit and into the street.

A quick backward glance showed Irene's advancing form, the top of her head floating eerily several inches above the others. Panic reached down Jazzy's throat and clutched her lungs in a steely fist. What if Derrick and the sheriff were wrong? What if Irene was the killer after all? She'd admitted to being in the Executive Inn last Friday night. Her threat-laced voice as she insisted that her daughter deserved to win the pageant rang vividly in Jazzy's ears. Had she tried to convince Josh Kirkland to vote for Heidi, and he'd refused? Did she want the Little Princess crown for her daughter badly enough to kill him? Maybe in hopes of better luck with his replacement?

The mass pressing around Jazzy was starting to thin out as people diverted to the tents and booths that lined the street. Fear whispered urgently in her ear. But she was safe in a crowd. Irene couldn't hurt her in the middle of a mob of festival-goers like those just ahead of her. She pushed forward, elbowing her way into the relative protection of the multitude that sauntered down Main Street. A drop of sweat slid down the side of her face, and she brushed it away.

Derrick was wrong about Irene, she was sure of it. Which meant he was wrong about Bradley, too. A horrible thought occurred to her. What if Irene had done something to Bradley? She'd left the Little Princess Pageant for a while this afternoon. Surely that wasn't normal. She'd want to see the other girls' talents, check out Heidi's competition. Had she slipped into his office, or maybe called him up to her room to answer a phony complaint?

Jazzy felt Irene's presence like the cold edge of a knife pressing against the back of her damp neck. She turned her head and glanced behind her. Irene was gaining. Pulse pounding in her ears, Jazzy pushed through the mob, going as fast as she could in the press of people that bloated the festival route. The protection of the crowd became a suffocating crush, hindering her ability to escape the woman who was gaining on her with every step.

Should she get out of the crowd, maybe make a dash for the grassy strip that ran alongside the river? Irene was strong, her muscles toned from years of working on the farm. But Jazzy was small and light, and she could run like the wind if she had to.

Especially if she was running for her life.

The brick buildings that marked the end of Main Street loomed ahead of her. She was almost at the end of the route. The dark alley that ran between those buildings beckoned like a gaping black hole just behind the last of the three-sided festival tents. Maybe she could duck in there and hide. With a burst of energy, she pushed through the crowd, crouching low so Irene couldn't see her, and dashed between two craft tents.

For a moment Jazzy thought she had succeeded. She hopped across the sidewalk and collapsed against the brick building to catch her breath.

When she looked up, her heart thudded to a stop.

Irene stepped between the tents, panting. The anger in her eyes slashed into Jazzy's terrified gaze.

Derrick rushed into the fellowship hall, clutching Jazzy's ensemble brochure in his hand. He forced himself to assume a calm appearance as he scanned the room for Sheriff Maguire. No sense making a scene at Chelsea's wedding.

There. The sheriff stood in the opposite corner of the room, his back presented to the reception guests. A hand cupped one ear while a finger plugged the other one. Derrick glimpsed a cell phone in his hand when he ducked his head.

Derrick strode across the room, dodging knots of people standing on the edges watching a line of dancers in the center do the Macarena. He'd almost reached the sheriff when a determined figure stepped in his path.

"Derrick Stephen, you haven't spoken to me all evening." Aunt Myrtle raised a wrinkled face toward him. "I have to leave tomorrow, you know, and given my precarious health this may be the last time you see me. Now help me over to my seat and let's have a nice, long chat about that violin player."

Derrick managed to keep the frustration out of his voice as he sidestepped his great aunt. "I'm sorry, Aunt Myrtle. I don't have time. I need to take care of something right now."

"Always in an all-fired hurry," he heard her mumble behind him.

He reached the sheriff as the man pulled the phone away from his ear and snapped the lid shut.

"Sheriff Maguire, we have to talk." Derrick lowered his voice, glancing around to make sure he was not overheard. "I know who killed Josh Kirkland."

"You'd better come with me, son." The eyes Maguire turned his way held a note of urgency Derrick had never seen. "Your girlfriend has gone missing."

"No use trying to run from me. I'll chase you to the ends of the earth if I have to." Irene advanced, each step like that of a stalking lion. "The least you can do is face me after what you done."

The rough brick pricked the skin on Jazzy's back through her silky blouse. "What do you mean? I didn't do anything."

Irene slitted her eyes. "They got to you, didn't they? Paid you off so's you'd vote for that tap-dancing rich girl."

Despite her fear, Jazzy's spine stiffened at the insult. "My vote was not for sale. I awarded the points I felt were fairly earned."

"Are you gonna stand right there and look me in the eye and tell me that girl's dancing was better than my Heidi's twirling?"

Jazzy gulped against a tight throat, but stood firm. "Yes, I am. Heidi's twirling was good, no doubt about it. But it was no better than the talents of at least half those other girls. And I'm sorry, but her interview question didn't even come close. She has no stage presence, and every other girl scored higher in poise and articulation."

"Mama?"

Irene's head whipped around as Jazzy's gaze snapped onto the figure that stepped between the two tents. Heidi had changed into jeans and a T-shirt, and most of the curls had wilted out of her limp brown hair. She still wore thick stage makeup, which looked horribly wrong on the face of a twelve-year-old.

"Heidi girl, what are you doing here? I told you to stay put back at the hotel."

The girl took another step toward them. "I'm sorry, Mama, but I thought you might be trying to talk to Miss Delaney, and I wanted to come, too." Her gaze slid to Jazzy's face for an instant before she ducked her head.

Jazzy felt terrible. Had the girl heard what she'd said about having no stage presence? Truthfulness was one thing, but injuring the tender feelings of a twelve-year-old was nothing short of cruel. "Heidi, I'm sorry I said that. I didn't know you were there or I would never have hurt your feelings."

"It's okay. Really. I know I didn't answer the question well. I tried, but I just…" The pathetic half-curls waved in the air as she shook her head.

Jazzy knew what she was trying to say. With a quick glance at Irene's face, she spoke to the girl. "You panicked when you got up there and saw all those people staring at you, didn't you?"

Shoulders drooping, her gaze fixed on the ground, Heidi nodded.

"I know exactly how you felt." Jazzy spoke gently, ignoring the mother and directing all her compassion toward the girl. "I have terrible stage fright, too. It's better now that I'm older, but my legs used to shake so badly I could hardly stand up. Sometimes everything went black and I was afraid I'd pass out right there in front of everyone."

Heidi looked up. "Yeah. That's happened to me, too."

"But you didn't pass out." Jazzy gave her an encouraging smile. "And when you started twirling your batons, you felt better, didn't you? Just like I do when I play my violin."

"Yeah, but—" Her mouth snapped shut as she cast a quick look at her mother. A struggle appeared on her face, and then she seemed to reach a decision. She straightened her shoulders and faced Irene. "But I don't want to do it again. I'm sorry, Mama. I don't want to be in any more pageants, and I don't want to audition for that modeling agency."

Irene's tone held a note of beseeching. "But Heidi girl, you got to do something to get yourself a break. You ain't gonna get stuck on no farm for the rest of your life, not whilst I got a breath left in my body."

"But I like farms. I like the animals. One day I'm going to be a veterinarian like Dr. Evans. I'm going to travel around the whole county and take care of farm animals, like he takes care of ours."

Irene shook her head. "But you gotta go to college for that. We don't have no money for college."

Jazzy took a step forward. "So maybe Heidi will get a scholarship. Or if not, there are grants and financial aid, even student loans. These days if someone wants a college education, there are all kinds of ways to get one." She smiled at the girl. "I think she'll make a great veterinarian. And she'll be much happier than she would be modeling."

Irene's expression held a lot of doubt, but the fierce anger had evaporated. As she watched the struggle in the tall woman's face, Jazzy's fear melted away.

Irene heaved a sigh. "Maybe we'd best be checking into them scholarships and things, then." Irene held out her arms, and Heidi stepped into them.

Forgotten, Jazzy watched as mother and daughter turned away and headed in the direction of the hotel. Turns out Derrick was right about one thing, anyway. This woman wasn't a killer. Hopefully he was still wrong about Bradley, though. But where *was* Bradley, anyway?

Lord, please keep him safe, and don't let him turn out to be the murderer.

She started to follow Irene and Heidi back to the hotel. But before she had taken two steps toward the opening between the tents, someone grabbed her from behind. A rough hand covered her mouth and muffled her scream as she was pulled into the dark alley.

TWENTY-FOUR

In the passenger seat of the sheriff's cruiser, Derrick clutched the brochure and tried not to stare at Jazzy's picture. Nausea threatened to choke him. The knowledge gnawed at his mind: Jazzy was missing. And he knew the identity of the killer.

"You saw the crowbar in that bag. I'll bet your lab will prove that's the one used to break into the hotel." He glanced sideways, where Sheriff Maguire's profile glowed an eerie green in the lights from the dashboard. "I'm telling you, the killer is Lester Kirkland."

"I'm not so sure about that." The sheriff's stubborn stare didn't edge Derrick's way.

"It's the only explanation that makes sense."

The sheriff shook his head once. His lips twisted as he chewed the inside of his cheek. Both hands gripped the steering wheel. "I shouldn't tell you this, but I will. My boys found a rope and half a dozen bottles of barbecue sauce in Goggins's office over at the Executive Inn. Same brand we found in the girls' hotel room. Same brand as on Kirkland's body. The rope had sauce smears on it, and it's the same diameter as the one the killer used to strangle Kirkland. That's what they came to the church to tell me."

"So you think Bradley's the killer?"

"The evidence seems to point that way, doesn't it?"

Derrick stared through the windshield. His rigid backbone felt like it would shatter if they hit a bump in the road. Blue-and-red lights from the top of the cruiser illuminated the darkness in a staccato pattern. Their strobelike flashes reflected off the clapboard sides of the houses they passed. Sheriff Maguire was trying to miss the rerouted downtown streets by navigating through the surrounding neighborhoods.

"Les could have planted it there to throw suspicion on Bradley." Derrick's stomach churned. Jazzy was right about Bradley all along. And the guy had been missing for several hours. They'd find his body somewhere. The sickness in his gut said so. Maybe they'd have to drag the river, but Les had killed Bradley, just like he'd killed his brother.

And Jazzy was missing.

He twisted in his seat to face the sheriff. "Listen, Les had access to the church storage room this morning. He told me himself he was in there early, setting up the tables and chairs for the wedding reception. He obviously had that bag with him when he broke into the girls' hotel room last night. That's when he picked up the brochure."

The sheriff continued to look unconvinced, but at least he didn't argue. Derrick went on. "And here's another thing that fits. You'll have to check it out, but I'll bet Les was the one who set up the meeting room last Friday night for the fishing tournament. You know yourself he picks up odd jobs like that all over town. Which would put him in the hotel Friday night, and again Saturday to set everything back the way it was."

Derrick sucked in a breath as another puzzle piece snapped into place. "I'll bet you anything Bradley hires Les to do the setup for a lot of the meetings that take place at the hotel. It would be cheaper than keeping somebody on staff full-time. And running in and out of the hotel on an official job would give Les access to the card encoder and the office key at the front desk."

Sheriff Maguire's expression softened a fraction. "That does make sense." His glance met Derrick's. "If that's the way it went down, you think Goggins figured it out?"

"He must have. He told Jazzy and me that he was positive the killer couldn't be one of his employees. But Les isn't really considered an employee. He's temporary help." Their conversation with Bradley replayed itself in his mind. "Bradley must have put it all together, and decided to confront Les."

The sheriff's head bobbed in a slow nod. "If that's the case, then we're going to have another body on our hands soon."

"I'm afraid so." Derrick straightened in his seat and stared through the window. "The only thing I can't figure out is why Les would be after the girls. Why break into their hotel room and strangle Liz?"

"I think I can explain that. It had to do with that picture on your girlfriend's cell phone."

Derrick looked at him. "The one of the pageant mother?"

Sheriff Maguire nodded. "She wasn't the only person in that picture. There was somebody else in the background, somebody wearing a baseball cap. Hard to see on that little screen. The image was fuzzy, and partially obstructed, but I have a feeling when the lab gets that picture analyzed we're going to see the face of the killer." He executed a turn, and finally Derrick glimpsed the hotel looming in front of him as the sheriff continued. "So Miss Delaney might have been right. The intruder wasn't after her friend. He was after the dark-haired girl who snapped that picture."

Tendrils of horror seeped into Derrick's mind. "Jazzy was right. He was after her. And now she's missing."

Jazzy huddled against the passenger door in the front seat of Les Kirkland's pickup. The night air blowing through a crack in the rear window held no trace of the festival fire pits. Instead, Jazzy whiffed the pungent odor of skunk as the truck veered around the curvy country roads. That, and the faint hint of French fries coming from one of the bags that had been wadded up and tossed onto the pile of garbage at her feet. She couldn't help but compare this truck with Derrick's. To think she'd turned her nose up at one lousy bag. Never again would she accuse someone of being dirty unless the trash was piled six inches deep, as it was here. And she was wearing open-toed shoes. *Shudder.*

The seat cushion on which Jazzy sat was ripped and filthy. She tried to compress her body into as small a space as possible, folding her shoulders forward so her bare arms wouldn't touch the dirty seat back. The duct tape with which her wrists had been bound in front of her was so tight it was cutting off the circulation in her hands. Her fingers were icy.

She risked a sideways glance. Les drove with one hand on the steering wheel, the other draped over the gearshift knob. He absently tapped his fingers in time with the country-and-western song playing on the radio.

"Where are you taking me?" Fear made her voice brittle.

"Out in the country a piece."

"And then—" Her voice cracked. She cleared her throat and tried again. "What are you going to do with me?"

He didn't answer, just turned to look at her. The pity she saw in his face turned the last shred of hope she held to despair. He was going to kill her, just like he'd killed his brother. Just like he'd probably killed Bradley. She shrank as far away from him as she could.

Lord, I don't want to die.

She was too young to die; her life had barely begun. There were so many things left undone. She'd never been to Europe. Never played Carnegie Hall. Never had children. Tears pooled in her eyes and she blinked them away. She, who had played the wedding march for so many others, would never hear it played at her own wedding.

Was there any chance she would be rescued? Surely her friends were looking for her. No doubt Matt had called the sheriff. Maybe he had put out an APB, closed the roads. And Derrick was with the sheriff at the wedding. Derrick would try to find her, wouldn't he?

Long white beams from the headlights cut through the darkness in front of the truck. The last house they'd passed had been several miles back. Trees lined the road on both sides. They were really out in the country, miles and miles from Waynesboro. Despondent, Jazzy realized if the sheriff and Derrick were looking for her, they would be searching in town. Probably in the hotel. He would question Irene for sure, and she would tell him about their conversation. At least she would pinpoint Jazzy's last known location for the searchers.

She swallowed, her throat swollen with tension. They would focus their search on the festival route. They wouldn't have any reason to look for her way out here in the country. If only she could send them a message, let them know where she was.

Her leg pressed against the passenger door, a lump from her pocket gouging into her thigh. Derrick's cell phone.

A light of hope flared as an idea flickered in her mind. If she could get that phone out of her pocket, she could call someone. Let them know where she was. Or at least who she was with.

Her hands had been bound in front of her, crossed at the wrists. If she could manage to work the phone out of her pocket with her left hand, she might be able to keep it hidden.

Jazzy edged her hands across her lap. Slowly, slowly. No quick movements or Les might notice. She kept glancing his way, praying as hard as she knew how that he wouldn't look at her.

He didn't. Her nerves jangled in rhythm with her pounding heart as she cupped the phone inside her pocket. These slacks were loose, the fabric slick and silky. A slight shift of her weight and the phone slid easily to the opening.

In her peripheral vision, she saw Les take his eyes off the road to glance at her. Hope grasped tightly in her left hand, Jazzy forced herself to be still and endure the weight of his stare.

"I didn't want to hurt you, you know. That wasn't part of my plan."

"You don't have to hurt me now. You could let me go."

The light inside the truck cab was dim. Jazzy hadn't taken the time to look at Derrick's phone. It felt the same size as hers. If it was a similar model, the screen would light up when she flipped open the cover. She edged her bound arms as far to the side away from Les as she dared. Maybe she could block most of the light with her body.

"I wish I could. I really do." He looked over at her. Jazzy froze and forced herself to return his gaze. "But I can't take the chance. You know what I done."

"I won't tell anybody. Honest. I'll carry your secret to my grave." *Lord, forgive me. I just lied with what will probably be one of my last breaths.*

His shoulders heaved in a silent laugh. "You're gonna do that anyway, ain't you?"

Ice invaded her veins at his callous tone. He was going to kill her way out here in the middle of nowhere. Would he cover her in barbecue sauce as he had done his brother? She flipped open the cell phone cover and pressed it immediately into her hip to douse the light. The brief flash shone like a beacon in her eyes, but Les didn't look her way. He must not have noticed.

One step closer to rescue.

Though she knew the odds against her were phenomenal,

Jazzy couldn't help warming herself in the hopeful blaze that flared within her. With chilly fingers, she investigated the keypad. It felt just like hers. Encouraged, she counted down the keys on the right side. Three, six, nine. She held her breath and pressed the nine. No sound. Derrick had the key tone turned off. Either that, or she was pushing the wrong button. Her finger slid across the keypad to what she hoped was the one, and she pressed it twice. Then she reached for the key above the one. If Derrick's phone was like hers, that button would connect her call.

She sent a mental request heavenward, and pressed the button.

TWENTY-FIVE

The flashing lights on the sheriff's car attracted stares from the horde of people walking through the parking lot toward the festival route. Derrick glanced at his watch. The Miss Bar-B-Q Pageant must have just ended. His nerves were strung tight as a bear trap, and these people sauntering across the pavement in their way were about to spring the hair trigger.

The sheriff's patience had apparently reached its limit as well. He reached for a dial on the dashboard. The car's siren let out a piercing *whoop-whoop*. People scattered, and he stomped on the gas pedal. The cruiser zoomed to the hotel's covered entryway.

The minute they skidded to a stop, Derrick jerked open the door and made a dash for the entrance. He was dimly aware that the sheriff followed him through the automatic doors at a more sedate pace, but Derrick wasn't about to stop and wait for him. He ignored the startled glances he drew as he dashed through the lobby toward Jazzy's suite.

As Derrick pounded on the door, the sheriff rounded the corner at the end of the hallway. The door opened, and Derrick looked into the miserable face of Matt Farmer.

"Derrick, I don't know what to say. I let her get away from me. I tried to stop her, but she wouldn't listen."

Derrick grabbed the deputy's upper arms in a firm grip. He

glared into Matt's face and gave him a shake. "Where? Tell me where she went."

Sheriff Maguire came up behind him and placed a restraining hand on Derrick's shoulder. "That's not going to help, son." He spoke in a low, even tone. "We're not going to find her by panicking. We need to keep level heads."

Derrick closed his eyes. The sheriff was right. He had to stay calm. *Lord, I need an extra dose of peace right now.*

He relaxed his grip on Matt's arms and opened his eyes. "I'm sorry, Matt."

"It wasn't his fault." Caitlin stood behind him, her arms hugging her body. She looked at Derrick through haunted eyes. "He really did try to stop her. But you know Jazzy."

Yes, Derrick was beginning to know her. A more headstrong, stubborn woman had never existed. But that stubbornness was merely a symptom of an iron will that ran deep, into her very soul. That core of iron was what made Jazzy so strong, so independent. So appealing.

And maybe that unbendable determination would serve her well now. *Hang on, Jazzy. We'll figure out a way to find you, but you've got to hang on.*

"9-1-1 dispatch, what—"

Jazzy let out a hacking cough, hopefully loud enough to drown out the woman's voice on the phone. When Les looked sharply her way, she pressed the phone more firmly into her thigh and doubled over, coughing as though she was choking on a fish bone.

"What's wrong with you?" His eyelids narrowed suspiciously as he stared at her.

"What's wrong with me?" Jazzy shouted. Hopefully her volume would serve the dual purpose of drowning out the dispatcher's voice, and also would alert the woman of her situation. "I've been kidnapped and I'm going to be murdered by the barbecue killer, that's what's wrong with me."

"Yeah, but I ain't choking you. What are you coughing like that for?"

"I don't know. I'm scared, and my throat is all tight because *I've been kidnapped and I'm going to die.*"

"Quit your yelling or I'll kill you right now!" Les matched her volume.

Jazzy snapped her mouth shut. She stared at him through wide eyes from which she didn't bother to hide her terror.

A hint of something flickered across his face. Nothing as strong as remorse, but a flash of compassion, maybe? The pickup lurched sideways on the road as he leaned forward to rummage in the litter on the floor by her feet. When he straightened, he tossed something onto the seat beside her leg. "There. That'll help your cough. I have to kill you, but you don't have to die with a dry throat."

Jazzy stared at a half-full bottle of spring water. Her stomach quivered. He had just pulled it from a pile of trash, and he had obviously drunk from it sometime in the past. No telling how long the germs from his saliva had been growing in the liquid that remained. If she were dying of dehydration in the middle of a desert, she couldn't force herself to drink that water.

"No, thank you. I'll pass."

"Okay, from the top." Sheriff Maguire sat in a chair, his elbows resting on the round table, fingers steepled. He peered at Matt, who sat across from him. "How did you lose her?"

Derrick stood watching from the kitchen, arms folded across his chest as he leaned against the counter. Liz and Caitlin huddled close together on the couch, fear for their friend plain on their faces.

Another deputy, a guy named Kenneth with whom Derrick shared a nodding acquaintance, hovered near the barred patio doors.

Matt's throat moved as he gulped. "She ran off. Said she'd left her planner in the room where the pageant was. I tried to stop her, but she got her dander up and took off before I could do anything. And I couldn't chase her down because I had to watch those two." He nodded toward Caitlin and Liz.

In the rational part of his mind, Derrick could sympathize with Matt's dilemma. Given the decision to chase down an uncooperative woman who was obviously unwilling to let him do his job, or stand guard over two compliant ones, he probably would have chosen the same. If the uncooperative woman had been anyone but Jazzy, that is.

The sheriff's fingers tapped against each other. "When you questioned Mrs. Baldwin, did she say why Miss Delaney ran outside?"

"She said it was obvious Miss Delaney was running from her. She thought it was because she was afraid of being accused of dishonesty in the Little Princess Pageant. But I figure Miss Delaney was scared, because she thought Mrs. Baldwin was the killer we've been looking for."

Sheriff Maguire nodded. "And Mrs. Baldwin says she left Miss Delaney in front of the First National Bank building at the other end of Main Street."

"That's right."

Kenneth spoke up from across the room. "We've got two men searching that area right now."

Frustration filled Derrick's gut like a gasoline-soaked rag just waiting to explode. Kenneth's comment came close to providing the spark. "Just two?" he snapped.

"That's everybody on duty."

"Call in the others." Sheriff Maguire issued the order through clenched teeth. "Nobody's off duty until we find this girl." He dropped his forehead forward to rest on his fingertips and heaved an audible sigh. "And notify the state police. Much as I hate having the state boys messing around in my jurisdiction, we need all the help we can get right now."

"Frank's up in Mrs. Baldwin's room, getting a written statement, but soon as he's finished—" Matt snapped his mouth shut when the sheriff's cell phone rang.

Maguire unclipped the phone from the waistband of his tux and held it to his ear. "Maguire." He paused. Even across the room Derrick heard an excited female voice, though he couldn't make out the words. "Put it through."

For a moment the sheriff didn't move. Then his head snapped up. His wide eyes sought first Matt's and then Kenneth's. "Y'all need to hear this. I'm putting it on speaker."

He punched a key on his cell phone and laid it on the table in front of him.

Derrick jerked upright when he heard the voice coming through the phone's tiny speaker. Jazzy's voice.

TWENTY-SIX

"Where are you taking me?"

Jazzy had no idea if the person on the other end of the cell phone could hear her or not. She had tucked the phone's cover beneath her leg to hide the screen's light and to muffle the sound. The bottom half was unobstructed, but it was on the other side of the truck cab from Les. The radio speaker in the door was right beside her knee, less than twelve inches from the phone. For all she knew, the only sound the 9-1-1 dispatcher could hear was Merle Haggard crooning, "The Bottle Let Me Down."

And if she had accidentally pressed the end key and disconnected the call, nobody could hear anything.

Les gave a humorless laugh. "You in a hurry to get there?"

Her heart flip-flopped at the reminder of the fate that waited for her when they reached their destination. "No, but I'd kind of like to know how long I have left."

"It ain't far now."

Tears sprung to Jazzy's eyes. If they didn't have far to go, how would the sheriff and Derrick ever find her? She had to give them some sort of clue, just in case someone was actually listening to this conversation.

"We're miles and miles from Waynesboro, way out in the country. All I can see are trees." That wasn't going to be much help. If only she knew which direction they were heading in. If only they would pass a street sign.

Les gave her a suspicious look. "Yeah. So?"

Blood roared through the veins in her ears. The throbbing sound made it hard to concentrate. She had to keep him talking. Any clue she could feed the people who might be listening would improve her chances of being rescued.

"They're not in town." The sheriff pointed at Kenneth. "Call the dispatcher on your phone. Get every available car out there. I want every road in the county covered, and I want it five minutes ago."

Kenneth unclipped his cell phone from his belt and stepped away to make the call. Derrick and the others huddled around the dinette table, all of them staring at the sheriff's cell phone. Tears glittered in Caitlin's eyes, and Liz's lips were pressed so tightly together they'd gone white. Derrick leaned both hands on the table and exchanged a nervous glance with Matt.

Keep talking, Jazzy. Tell us where you are.

"Uh, can I ask a question, Mr. Kirkland? Why did you kill your brother?" There. If anybody was listening, they knew who had kidnapped her.

"It's a long story."

She managed a feeble smile. "The longer the better, if you ask me."

He put his head back and laughed. "You're a funny girl. Smart, too. You gotta be smart to play a fiddle, I guess."

Violin. Jazzy bit back the correction. She did not want to waste what might be her last minutes talking about how smart she was. Smart girls did not run away from the deputy guarding them.

"Your brother?" she prompted. "Did he make you mad somehow?"

Les's jaw bunched, and his grip on the steering wheel tightened. "All the time."

"When we talked this morning I got the impression you sort of looked up to him."

A blast of disgust sprayed drops of spittle on the windshield. "Everybody looked up to Josh. All through school, he's the one everybody was proud of. The big football player. The one everybody wanted to sit by at lunchtime. Nobody wanted to sit with me, but he made 'em. Used to tell 'em, 'If you want to hang out with me, you have to hang out with my big brother, too.'"

"That was nice of him."

Jazzy shrank at the vicious gaze he turned toward her. "Yeah, everybody thought so, him included. But he let me know what a big favor he was doing me. And he let Momma know, too. Momma was always proud of her baby." Bitterness rasped through his voice.

"More proud of him than of you?" Jazzy spoke softly.

He didn't answer at first. Both hands gripped the steering wheel. The glare he directed toward the road in front of the truck chilled Jazzy's blood.

"Ain't right to treat one young 'un better'n t'other. But it weren't Momma's fault. Josh was smart right from the cradle. He had her so's she'd do whatever he wanted. But he went too far." He shook his head, his eyes unfocused. "He went too far."

The road dipped and then curved sharply to the right. Jazzy was thrown against the door. To her horror, the phone slipped from beneath her thigh and skittered to the floor, where it disappeared beneath the pile of trash.

They heard a loud noise, and the phone line went dead.

"No!"

Derrick jerked forward and reached for the cell phone, but the sheriff beat him to it. He snatched it up and checked the display.

"She's gone."

His words fell like blows. Derrick sank into the nearest chair. One part of his brain knew that Maguire meant the connection was gone, but he couldn't shake the feeling of doom those words portended.

"Can't they trace the call and find out where she is?" Caitlin's voice trembled.

Sheriff Maguire shook his head. "It's a cell phone. The only address we can get is the billing address. Unless it has a GPS?"

He glanced at Derrick, who dropped his head onto his arms. If only he'd upgraded his phone, paid the extra bucks and got one of those fancy ones with all the gadgets. "No GPS."

The phone rang, and hope flared in the midst of Derrick's despair. Had she managed to call back?

The sheriff looked at the screen and shook his head. "It's the dispatch office." He flipped open the lid. "Maguire." Pause. "No! Don't call her back. If Kirkland doesn't know she has a phone we don't want to clue him in. Did you get a recording of that call?" Pause. "Yeah, well I want you and everybody else over there to listen to it again. Over and over. See if you can hear anything in the background that will give us an idea of their location." Another pause. Sheriff Maguire lifted his eyes toward the ceiling. "Yes, just like on *CSI*. Call me if you find anything."

When he snapped the lid shut, his jaw squared. He straightened and spoke with authority. "Okay, people, there's a lot we don't know. Let's focus on what we do know. They're in a vehicle and they're out in the country."

The man's take-charge attitude enabled Derrick to hold the nearly overpowering despair at bay. He raised his head and steeled his voice against the tide of emotion. "Les drives a pickup. Older-model Ford. Sky-blue with a fair amount of rust."

Derrick remembered seeing it earlier, loaded down with chairs for the makeshift stage the man had been setting up.

"Good." Maguire pointed at Kenneth. "Get the tag number and have it broadcast to every law-enforcement officer in the state."

"But what if Kirkland has a police scanner? He'll hear the broadcast and know we're onto him."

The sheriff sat silently for a moment, chewing on the inside of his cheek. Then he slapped a flat hand on the table. "It's a chance we've got to take. We need to find him before he hurts that girl."

Kenneth nodded and stepped to the far corner to make another call.

"What else?" Sheriff Maguire's gaze circled those at the table. "How many roads head out of Waynesboro?"

"There's four hundred and sixty square miles in this county, and more roads than we can count," Matt said. "We need a detailed map like the one on the wall down at headquarters. Maybe we ought to go down there."

The sheriff shook his head. "We don't have time. We have to move now. Come on, we know our own county, every mile of it. Since Miss Delaney was last seen on Main Street, let's start with the roads leading out of town. Name them."

"U.S. 60," Liz said. "That's the road we came to town on."

Maguire shot an approving glance at her. "Good. And there's the parkway, but neither of those have trees. The girl said she saw trees."

"There's State Road 121, and 431," Matt said, "but it's mostly farmland out that way. What about 231?"

Derrick fixed his gaze on the ceiling and tried to build a map of the county in his mind. "Or County Road 56, or 54, or 81. Lots of deep woods out on 81."

Maguire shot out of his chair, his eyes wide. "That's it.

Kirkland's mother owns property out on Masonville Road, a couple miles off of 81. We went out there yesterday to break the news of her son's death."

Derrick caught some of the man's excitement, but doubt niggled at him. "You don't think he'd take Jazzy to his mother's house to kill her, do you?"

"Nah, I don't." Sheriff Maguire shook his head. "But you said it yourself. There's acres and acres of woods out there. A body dumped out in those woods would stay hidden for a long, long, time. And Kirkland grew up in those woods. Nobody knows them better."

Derrick's hopes sank. How could they ever find Jazzy in miles and miles of dense trees? They could wander for days looking for her.

"Bloodhounds!" The chair crashed to the floor behind him when he jumped out of it. "Bloodhounds could find her."

"We don't have trained dogs." Matt looked at the sheriff. "But we could call over to Davis County, maybe borrow theirs. It'll take them a while to get here, though."

Maguire nodded. "Do it."

Derrick saw a flicker of hope in Liz's eyes. She was thinking the same thing as he was.

He rounded on the sheriff. "I've got an idea. I need to get back to the church."

TWENTY-SEVEN

"What do you mean he went too far? What did Josh do?"

Jazzy had no idea if the cell phone on the floor was still transmitting. She searched for it by sifting through the disgusting collection of bags and cans and who-knew-what-else with her feet, trying to move as unobtrusively as possible. She needed to keep Les talking so he didn't notice what she was doing.

"It ain't what he done. It's what he planned to do. My momma ain't gonna be with us much longer. She's got a weak heart, and she can't stay away from the sweets even though the doctor told her the sugar's gonna kill her." His finger stabbed at the dashboard. "Josh knew that, and he was pushing her to leave her property to him. Said I didn't know nothing about tending a property and taxes and all, and he'd take care of me, make sure I didn't want for nothing. She believed him. She was aiming to make a will after the festival."

Jazzy's toe came in contact with something hard. It might be the phone. She maneuvered her feet to position the object between them, trying hard not to think about the germs her bare toes were undoubtedly coming in contact with.

"How did you find out about the will?"

"Momma told me. Said she wanted me to know, so's if anything happened to her I wouldn't worry because Josh would take care of me." Les's expression turned grim. "But I know what he was planning. He talked about it before. It bugged him that Momma just let all that land run to wild when she could make it pay. He was gonna parcel that property off, every acre, and sell it to some developer from up north. Then he'd make a bundle, and I'd get stuck with nothing." He tilted his head back, chin high. "Well, now it'll be mine, and I ain't gonna let no developer within fifty miles of the place."

"So you killed him and covered his body in barbecue sauce to make the sheriff think his death was connected to the festival." Exactly like Sheriff Maguire said. Jazzy hoped he was listening.

He glanced her way. Jazzy halted the movement of her feet until he faced the road again. "See, I knew you was smart. I'm pretty smart myself. I wore a disguise and everything. I stayed clear of anybody who worked at the hotel who might recognize me that day, and if any strangers happened to notice me they'd tell the sheriff it was some guy with a ponytail. Everything was going just fine until you and your friends showed up snapping pictures."

"So you broke into our room to get the camera. Why didn't you kill us then?"

"Not the camera." He looked at her. "Your phone. You snapped a picture right when I was walking by, and you looked right at my face. I knowed I had to shut you up. But last night I got the wrong girl by the throat. It shook me. I let go and made a run for it. Shouldn't 'a done that."

"But I didn't see you in the hotel lobby. Honest."

He shook his head. "I ain't about to believe that. When you and that Rogers boy came upon me today down by the river, I saw it in your eyes. You recognized me. Maybe you couldn't put a finger on exactly where you knew me from, but you'd figure it out soon enough. I couldn't take that chance."

A knot of tears clogged Jazzy's throat. She was about to be

killed for something she'd never seen. "No, really, I didn't see you at the hotel. I recognized you from the church."

Kirkland studied her through narrowed lids for a moment. Then he lifted a shoulder. "Well, even if you didn't know before, you do now."

Jazzy finally managed to maneuver the hard object between her sandaled feet. She could feel it with her big toes, the battery still warm. Disappointment stabbed through her chest. The cover had snapped closed. Nobody was hearing the conversation.

Her only hope now was to try to talk Les out of killing her. A barely suppressed sob shook her voice. "The sheriff took my phone. Mr. Kirkland, if you let me go, maybe he'll go easier on you. But if you kill me you'll be convicted for two murders instead of one."

He turned his head. The darkness inside the truck turned his eyes into black pits. "Three."

Bradley. The sob broke loose. Her chest heaved with it. "What did you do with Bradley?"

"You'll see."

Frightened tears wet her cheeks. He was taking her out to the place where he'd killed Bradley so he could kill her, too. One of the last things she'd see this side of heaven would be the corpse of a man she'd come to think of as a friend.

She wasn't going to be able to talk Les out of killing her. Terror threatened to choke her. There'd never been a situation she couldn't manage to get out of. When she'd faced and conquered her stage fright, Jazzy had realized she could handle anything. College. Finding a good job. Putting together the ensemble. Any challenge that came her way, no matter how hard. She took pride in her independence, her self-sufficiency. That's why Derrick's attempts at protecting her had rubbed her the wrong way.

But what good was pride in the last moments of life? Right now she'd give anything for Derrick's protection.

"Have you been following me all day, waiting for the chance to kidnap me?" Her breath shuddered as she sniffed.

"Funny thing about that." Les maneuvered the truck around another curve. "I was planning to follow you back home and get you there. But tonight, when I was walking along the river back at the festival, waiting for that bluegrass band to finish so's I could put the chairs up, who do I see running through the crowd?" The grin he turned her way was more like a leer. "You. I slipped around the bank building and hid in the alley, waiting to see what you was doing. Heard you talking with the Baldwin woman. And then I saw my chance. I ain't never been one to let a chance go by."

The truck slowed, and Les turned the wheel to maneuver between the trees onto a narrow dirt path Jazzy hadn't even seen. She saw no lights, no houses, nothing but trees all around. The moon's white light didn't penetrate through the branches. All around her was nothing but blackness. The truck bumped and bucked, taking her deeper into the woods.

And then they came to a sudden stop. Les cut the engine and looked at her.

God, please do something. I don't want to die!

Derrick folded his hands together beneath his chin and pleaded, "Mrs. Kirkland, you've got to help us. Where would Les go if he wanted to hide something?"

The old woman sat on a dingy sofa, a metal walker within reach. Her broad face wore a dazed expression as she stared at the worn carpet. "I cain't believe it. My Lester done kilt my Joshua."

Compassion warred with the urgency in Derrick's gut. He wanted to take her by the shoulders and shake the information out of her, but her lost stare kept him on the other side of the room.

Sheriff Maguire stood beside him in the tiny living room, still wearing his tuxedo pants and ruffled shirt. "Ma'am, I can't imagine how you must be feeling. I'm truly sorry to bring this news to you, but we need your help. A young woman's life is at stake."

Hands clasped in her lap, she shook her head with a slow movement that stirred Derrick's heart. "I want to help you, I do. But I ain't been out on the property in a coon's age. I cain't for the life of me think where he'd hide something."

This poor woman. Derrick thought of his own mother, of her flushed face as she'd laughed up at him a few short hours ago. He remembered her grief when Dad had passed away. What must this mother be going through? She'd just lost one son, and now they were telling her that the only person she had left in the world was responsible. No comfort he could offer would ever be enough.

Derrick crossed the floor in one long stride and knelt before her. He covered her hands with one of his. "Mrs. Kirkland, do you mind if I pray with you?"

He felt the sheriff's impatience behind him as he shifted his weight from one foot to the other. Derrick ignored him and focused instead on smiling as compassionately as he could manage into the tortured, watery eyes in front of him.

She nodded.

Derrick bowed his head. "Lord, Mrs. Kirkland's pain is deep, and we don't know how to comfort her. But You do. Your Son died, too, so You know what she's going through. I'm asking You to give her the comfort only You can. And if there's anything she can tell us that will help us find Jazzy, please bring it to the front of her mind. Amen."

Mrs. Kirkland gave a gigantic sniff as Derrick squeezed her hands. "Thank you. I appreciate that. But I don't have nothing in the front of my mind that can help you find that girl."

Derrick did not let the stab of disappointment show on his face.

"Are there any structures on the property?" Sheriff Maguire

asked. "A cabin, maybe, or even a clearing where Les might pitch a tent on occasion?"

"Nah, we never built nothing 'cept this here house." She pursed her lips. Then a flash of remembrance crossed her face. "My husband built him a deer blind a year before he died. I never give it no thought for years, but Lester mentioned it last deer season. I was surprised it was still standing."

Derrick stood. A thrill zipped through his core. This was the place they were looking for, he was certain of it. "Do you remember where it is?"

She nodded and lifted a hand to point. "Back up the road a piece you'll find a pull-off. No more than a dirt path, really. The deer blind is about a half mile straight back through the woods from there."

Derrick remembered to thank her as he dashed out the door to the sheriff's cruiser.

TWENTY-EIGHT

"Come on. We have to walk a piece from here."

Thoughts and alarm whirled together in Jazzy's mind. Now that the truck had stopped, she could make a run for it. Her hands were taped together, but not her feet. The black clothes she was wearing would render her nearly invisible in the dark woods. She just needed a minute's head start, a minute when he wasn't looking.

Les's door opened, and when he swung his feet outside, Jazzy made her move. She grabbed the door handle and jerked.

Nothing happened.

She jerked again, and again, panic rising like acid in her throat. Why wouldn't the door open?

A laugh behind her made her whirl around in her seat.

Les leaned down to look into the cab. "That handle broke a couple months ago. Only opens from the outside." He reached down and pulled out a rifle from behind the seat. "Scoot on over here and get out."

Tears flooded her eyes, and for a moment Jazzy couldn't see. "Please don't kill me." She choked out the words, her chest shuddering with sobs. Pride was nothing but a distant memory. She was desperate and begging for her life. "It won't do any good. If I did take a picture of you, the sheriff is going to see it on my phone. He'll know you're the murderer. My death will gain you nothing. Please, let me live."

Les leaned into the truck. "I didn't want to kill you, I really didn't. Nor Mr. Goggins, neither. But I got to. There's a chance I ain't in that picture. Or if I am, you might have got the back of my head. I turned just when you took it. Maybe I was quick enough." He grabbed her roughly by the arm and pulled her across the seat. "This is your own fault. If you and your friends had gone home after I broke into your room last night, none of this would have happened."

Should she tell him about the cell phone buried in the trash on the floorboard? Instinct told her to keep that secret. She knew now that nothing she could say would convince him to spare her life. She was going to die—he would not be persuaded otherwise. But there was still a slim chance the 9-1-1 operator had heard enough to identify Les. At least they would catch her killer.

Jazzy slid from the truck, dry leaves crunching beneath her feet when she landed. Moonlight filtered through the limbs overhead to cast weird patterns on his face, like eerie tribal-paint designs on his skin. His eyes held hers in an unrelenting vise. They glowed with determination. A shudder shook Jazzy's body. There was no arguing with that unyielding look.

Held captive by his unbreakable grip on her arm, Jazzy was pulled forward. She sobbed openly as she trudged. Prickly branches snagged at her clothes and scratched her bare arms. Damp dirt and dead leaves slipped into her shoes beneath her toes as she scuffed her feet, trying to prolong the inevitable. Pain throbbed in her arm where his fingers gouged the flesh. She twisted once, trying to shake his grip and make a dash for it, but he held tight.

And still they walked on.

* * *

Derrick sat in the front seat of the sheriff's cruiser, clutching the sweater Jazzy had left in his truck. Three deputies' vehicles formed a caravan behind them. In the backseat, Old Sue stood with her nose pressed to the window. He turned around to look at her. The dog's legs quivered as she peered into the darkness. Probably picking up tension from him.

"I hope this works," he told the sheriff.

Sheriff Maguire glanced into the rearview mirror. "It's the best chance we've got." His tone spoke volumes about his doubt.

Derrick struggled to maintain his composure. His feet wouldn't stop their nervous jiggling. "Shouldn't we have found that path by now?"

The sheriff gave a single nod, his eyes fixed on the road. "I hope we didn't miss it."

"Almost there now."

Jazzy stumbled over a dead branch and would have fallen if not for Les's grip on her arm. Her tears had stopped, dried up in the face of the terror that escalated with each step. She wanted to pray, but her numb mind couldn't form the words. The only prayer she could think of was the one her church repeated every Sunday morning. She spared a hope that God wasn't picky in situations like this.

Our Father, who art in heaven, hallowed be Thy name…

"Here we are."

Les jerked her to a stop. They stood in a small clearing, staring at a structure, made out of weathered wood planks, in the shape of a teepee around a tall tree. A narrow opening yawned on the side facing Jazzy, the inside pitch-black.

Les shoved her forward. "Get on in there. Your buddy's waiting for you."

A whimper escaped her trembling lips. He'd stashed Bradley's body in this little building out here in the middle of nowhere? And he wanted her to go in there and look at it?

A shrill scream pierced the night. Jazzy whirled around in time to see Les crash to his knees. He shook his head. Both hands gripped the rifle. It rose, the barrel pointing toward her.

Someone grabbed her blouse and jerked her sideways. A voice shouted in her ear, "Don't just stand there. Run!"

Jazzy ran.

TWENTY-NINE

"There!" Derrick stabbed a finger at the windshield.

"I see it." Sheriff Maguire yanked the cruiser with a sharp one-handed maneuver, his other hand reaching for his radio. "Maguire here. We're one-point-seven miles west of the Kirkland place, south side of the road."

Static crackled through the speaker for a second before the dispatcher responded. "Ten-four. We've got three KSP units en route to your location."

The cruiser bounced over the uneven ground. Stuttering blue and red lights gave the trees around them a spooky, carnival feel, like a house of horrors. Derrick gripped the armrest as they hit a jarring gouge in the forest floor, his gaze glued on the place where the headlights' twin beams sliced through the blackness.

He glimpsed something unnatural up ahead. Sky-blue steel looked whitish in the headlights. Red and blue flashes reflected off a metal bumper.

Les's pickup.

"Looks like we were right." The sheriff's unruffled tone sounded almost matter-of-fact.

How could he stay so calm while Derrick's pounding pulse stole his breath?

Before the cruiser came to a stop, Derrick jerked open the door and tumbled out. He opened the back door. "Come on, Old Sue."

The dog leaped to the ground. Her stiff brown tail vibrated nervously, and her legs trembled. Derrick led her around to the front of Les's truck and dropped down on one knee. He placed a hand on the back of her head and held Jazzy's sweater in front of her snout. "Girl, you remember Jazzy, don't you?"

Deputies piled out of cars behind him. Derrick ignored them and focused on speaking to his dog in an even tone.

Old Sue nosed the sweater, then extended her neck to wet his cheek with a warm tongue. Derrick pushed her gently back. "We're going hunting, Old Sue." He let her sniff the sweater once again, then stood. Looking down, he held the dog's gaze as he always did before issuing a command. Old Sue's hindquarters plopped to the ground and she sat at attention. Not a whisker moved. Derrick pointed toward the dense wooded area in front of the pickup. "Find Jazzy, girl. Hunt."

The dog leaped up on all fours. She hesitated, head turned in the direction he pointed. In the headlights from the sheriff's car Derrick saw her nose twitch, but she didn't move. Instead, she looked back at him, head cocked sideways, clearly questioning what he wanted her to do. A sinkhole opened somewhere in his chest and threatened to pull his heart into its despairing depths. She didn't understand what he was asking her to do.

Sheriff Maguire stepped up beside him. "She's not a trained bloodhound, son. You can't expect her to act like one." He looked up toward his watching deputies. "Okay, boys, spread out. Kenneth, you stay here and send the reinforcements after—"

A shot rang through the night.

Derrick's head jerked in the direction from which it came. *Dear God, no!*

Old Sue leaped forward and disappeared into the darkness.

* * *

Something zipped past her right shoulder. Wood splintered in the trunk of a tree as she ran by.

A bullet! He's shooting at me!

She twisted sideways to dash around another tree, following the figure that ran in front of her. The man was pulling away, the distance between them growing.

Sandals are not the best shoes for running in the forest.

Her brain skipped from thought to random thought.

And it's hard to run with my hands bound. Weird. You wouldn't think so.

Just ahead, the man glanced over his shoulder to gauge her position. She got a glimpse of his profile.

"Bradley!"

"Shhhhhh!"

Another shot from behind sent an adrenaline boost to her legs. Or maybe it was the thrill that zipped through her brain as she realized the incredible truth. Bradley was alive. Not dead. Not basted in barbecue sauce. Alive!

But Les was gaining on them. The noise of his feet crunching through the undergrowth behind her pierced the night. Her own ragged breathing sounded louder still. He was going to catch her. Any minute she would hear another shot, would feel the bullet tearing through the skin on her back.

Something zipped by her leg this time. Something white. Some kind of animal.

A vicious growl. Another gunshot.

Jazzy couldn't help it. She had to see what was happening. She turned her head—

—and smacked into something solid. She felt herself thrown backward. The ground embraced her with a thud, and a heavy weight crushed her. Breath was snatched from her lungs. White spots of light exploded in her eyes.

"Jazzy! Jazzy, are you all right?"

That voice she knew. Gulping air, she shook her head and looked up into the most gorgeous chocolate eyes in the entire world.

Relief poured through her body as air rushed back into her lungs. She buried her face in Derrick's chest, sobbing. "You found me! Thank God, you found me."

He rolled sideways, pulling her with him. His hands stroked her hair as he whispered in her ear, "That's exactly right. Thank You, God. Thank You for letting us find her in time."

THIRTY

Three of them huddled together in the back of the sheriff's cruiser. Bradley, exhausted from his ordeal, had collapsed against the passenger door in the front seat. Jazzy snuggled deeper beneath Derrick's arm and pulled Old Sue closer on her lap. The dog's bath was obviously wearing off. An unpleasant canine odor assaulted Jazzy's nostrils, but she chose to ignore it. Old Sue had risked her life when she had attacked a man holding a gun. Jazzy was prepared to put up with a lot of doggy smell.

Derrick's arm pulled her even closer within his protective embrace. A satisfied warmth spread through her body, chasing away the last of the fear-filled tremors. Turned out having someone to protect you wasn't all bad. In fact, she could get used to this.

The dog lifted her head and bathed Jazzy's face in slobber.

Jazzy's stomach lurched. Some things she could not force herself to get used to. She gave the snout a gentle shove. "Enough is enough. I don't know where that tongue has been, so keep it out of my face, okay?"

Derrick laughed, and Jazzy felt the rumble in his chest through her cheekbone.

"I don't understand one thing." Jazzy directed her voice toward the front seat. "Why didn't Les kill Bradley when he took him out in the woods? Why leave him tied up in that little building?"

Bradley spoke without lifting his head from the window. His words slurred with tiredness. "I thought about that in the hours I was duct-taped to that tree. The only thing I could come up with is that I surprised him. He wasn't prepared for me to figure out he was the killer. It probably took him a while to work himself up to killing his brother, and he never considered he'd have two victims. When he left me, he said something about having to take care of the chairs, but he'd be back."

"Maybe it's harder to kill a stranger than a blood relative," Derrick suggested.

Sheriff Maguire nodded. "There's something to that. He had a motive for killing his brother, and time to justify it in his mind. He told Miss Delaney he hesitated over killing her friend. Maybe he needed a while to justify three murders." He caught Jazzy's eye in the rearview mirror. "But I have no doubt he convinced himself it was necessary in the end."

Light flooded the cruiser as they pulled into the emergency-room entrance of the small Waynesboro hospital. Jazzy would have preferred to go back to the hotel, but the sheriff had insisted she get checked over. And Bradley had scraped off a significant amount of skin with several hours of rubbing the duct tape against rough tree bark to free himself. His forearms definitely needed medical treatment.

Jazzy reluctantly pulled herself away from the warmth of Derrick's body when Sheriff Maguire opened the door. Old Sue followed her owner, and Jazzy accepted Derrick's hand to help her out of the car.

In the next instant she was nearly knocked back inside when two bodies threw themselves at her.

"You're alive," Caitlin sobbed. "Thank You, Lord, thank You."

Liz crushed Jazzy's ribs in a hug, then pulled back with a mighty sniff. "You smell like dog." Her eyebrows arched as her gaze traveled down Jazzy's body. "And you're filthy. Look at your clothes, your arms." Her eyes widened as her gaze reached the ground. "Look at your feet!"

Jazzy looked down. Her toes were nearly black with dirt, and a twig protruded from the side of her right sandal. Her hands were filthy. Germs were probably swarming over her body. Liz was right; she couldn't remember the last time she'd been this grimy.

But she didn't care. It wasn't important.

She slipped an arm around Derrick's waist and lifted her face toward his. A thrill shot through her at the glimmer of love she saw shining in his eyes.

That was important.

She grinned at her friends. "Oh, what's wrong with a little dirt, anyway?"

EPILOGUE

The sun shone from a glorious blue sky and sparkled off the rapidly moving waters of the Kentucky River. Jazzy had forgotten to grab her sunglasses out of the car when she'd loaded her luggage for the trip back home. She squinted against the glare and shielded her eyes to watch Old Sue bound away from them toward the riverbank.

"What if she jumps in?" She allowed a note of worry to creep into her question. "That water's moving pretty fast."

Beside her, Derrick shook his head. "She won't. She's just enjoying the sunshine."

When the dog skidded to a stop at the edge of the grass, Jazzy lowered her hand and turned a smile up toward him. Derrick's arm tightened around her, pulling her close. The clean, fresh scent of his aftershave overrode the smoke from the barbecue pits, and Jazzy leaned in and breathed deeply.

"Excuse me."

She felt a tap on her shoulder. Liz and Caitlin had returned from their errand on the festival route carrying plastic grocery sacks full of barbecue and burgoo.

"I need to see some daylight between you two." A playful smile lurked around Caitlin's lips.

"Yeah, no smooching in public." Liz spoiled her schoolmarm scold with an indulgent grin.

Laughing, Derrick pulled away slightly, though he didn't release Jazzy. "Do you always travel with a pair of chaperones?"

Jazzy nodded. "No soloists in this group. We come as a trio."

"Though we're open to becoming a quartet," Caitlin told him. "Do you happen to play the viola?"

Derrick shook his head. "Trust me, you don't want me to try to play an instrument. As my Aunt Myrtle says, I have a tin ear."

Ah, but you're an expert at playing my heartstrings. Jazzy shut her mouth before the thought escaped. Liz would never let her hear the end of it if she showed what a sentimental sap she'd become practically overnight.

"So, did you get what you needed?" Jazzy nodded toward their bags.

"Sure did. Award-winning burgoo." Caitlin held up a heavy sack.

Liz scowled. "She even talked them into an extra quart for free when she bragged that she was one of the judges. A slick piece of extortion if you ask me."

"It's not extortion," Caitlin said. "The competition is over, so they have nothing to gain by buying my favor. They were just being nice because I told them how much better I thought theirs was than the other entries. You have to admit it's really good. You said so yourself."

Jazzy turned a disbelieving stare on Liz. "You actually tried roadkill stew?"

"They practically held me down and poured it into my mouth." Liz lifted a shoulder and admitted, "It wasn't bad, but I'll stick to the barbecue." She held a bulging bag of her own.

Old Sue bounded up to them, and Jazzy stooped to rub the dog's silky ears. She smelled better this morning. Apparently Derrick had given her another bath before bringing her over to say goodbye. Though Jazzy wouldn't have thought it possible three days ago, she was going to miss this dog.

And her owner.

She straightened, fighting to keep her face from showing the sudden melancholy that threatened to send tears into her eyes. "I think it's time we hit the road."

Caitlin and Liz headed toward the car. Derrick grabbed Jazzy's hand as they fell in step behind them, Old Sue sticking close. Jazzy reveled in the strength of his hand, the way it surrounded hers with his warmth. When they neared the car his step slowed, as though he dreaded the parting that was now upon them as much as she did.

Why, when she'd finally found the guy who made her pulse pound, did she have to live four hours away? *Lord, it's just not fair!*

They reached the car, and she tossed her keys to Liz so she and Caitlin could stash their purchases in the disposable cooler Bradley had given them when they'd checked out of the hotel.

"You know," Derrick told her, "now that Chelsea is married, my mom has a spare room. She told me to tell you that anytime you feel like spending a weekend in the country, you've got a place to stay."

"Really?" A tiny spark flickered in the dark mood that threatened to envelop her. *He talked to his mother about me?*

He grinned. "I might even teach you how to fish. And I have something for you. Wait here."

Caitlin and Liz climbed into the car. Jazzy leaned against the driver's-side door while Derrick dashed between two parked cars toward his pickup. When he returned, he held a box. As he neared, Jazzy saw that it was—

She looked up at him. "You bought me a new cell phone?"

He thrust the box into her hands. "Not only that, but I bought myself one, too, since the sheriff confiscated mine from the floor of Les's truck. I, uh…" A flush stained his cheeks, and he ducked his head. "I went by the store this morning and signed us up for the family plan. So we can talk to each other anytime for free."

A rush of joy propelled Jazzy forward, straight into Derrick's arms. "We'll talk every day," she mumbled against his shoulder.

"Five times a day," Derrick promised.

"And we'll see each other on weekends."

His chin moved against her head as he nodded. "Every weekend without fail."

"I'll miss you so much."

"Not as much as I'll miss you."

Liz's sarcastic voice sounded through the open car window behind Jazzy. "This is starting to sound like a bad country-and-western song. Just kiss him goodbye."

Jazzy couldn't hold back her giggle as she looked up into Derrick's face. "We'd best do as she says."

His face lowered toward hers and his voice purred in her ear. "With pleasure."

Jazzy closed her eyes and surrendered to his kiss, confident that there would be many more to follow.

* * * * *

Dear Reader,

Every year over Mother's Day weekend, Owensboro, Kentucky, hosts the International Bar-B-Q Festival. Several of the town's streets are closed to traffic and fill up with festival activities. I first went there almost twenty years ago, and that's where I tasted real Kentucky burgoo for the first time. Trust me—it's yummy! The festival attracts thousands of visitors from all over, and those cooking teams really do produce the best barbecue I've ever eaten.

I often get inspiration for my books from real places and events, but then I transform them into works of pure fiction, as I've done in *A Taste of Murder.* The competitions at the real International Bar-B-Q Festival are friendly, not nearly as intense as I've depicted in the fictitious contest in this book. The festival route is similar to my made-up one, complete with a hotel that hosts beauty pageants for a variety of ages. But that hotel is a lot nicer than the one in this book, and the pageant folks are a lot nicer, too.

Jazzy and Derrick are also based on an element of reality. I'm a musician—a singer. My husband, who was raised on a farm, loves to hunt and fish. But since we've found true love in one another, I'm confident that happily-ever-after is possible for my fictitious couple. I don't know about you, but I love happy endings, especially in murder mysteries!

Thanks for reading *A Taste of Murder.* I hope you'll let me know what you thought of my book.

Virginia Smith

QUESTIONS FOR DISCUSSION

1. Josh Kirkland, the victim in *A Taste of Murder,* isn't a very likable character. What behaviors did he choose to exhibit that may have led to his untimely end?

2. If you figured out who killed Josh Kirkland, when did you confirm your suspicion? If you didn't figure it out, who did you suspect?

3. Jazzy and Heidi Baldwin have something in common. What is it? How does this common bond affect Jazzy?

4. Jazzy has successfully overcome her stage fright by focusing on her real audience and striving to give God her best. Have you employed similar means to overcome a fear?

5. Derrick feels a sense of responsibility for Jazzy and her friends that goes beyond his invitation to play at his sister's wedding. Why?

6. Jazzy's near obsession with cleanliness is a form of perfectionism. What elements in her past may have led to the development of this personality trait?

7. During the story, Jazzy mentions her commitment to date only Christian men. Is this a reasonable commitment? Why, or why not?

8. Derrick and Jazzy initially met through an online social community when he inquired about hiring her musical

ensemble. What precautions did Jazzy take before agreeing to meet him in person? How should today's young people ensure their own safety in online communities?

9. The origins of Kentucky Burgoo can reportedly be traced back to the early 1800s, where it made its debut as "squirrel and wild-game stew." That may explain its tongue-in-cheek reputation as "roadkill stew." Does the area in which you live have regional recipes that might cause outsiders to raise their eyebrows?

10. Which character in *A Taste of Murder* do you most identify with? Why?

11. When the story opens, Jazzy isn't crazy about animals. How does Old Sue win her over?

12. Do you have a favorite pet? Discuss your favorite pet story.

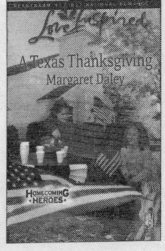

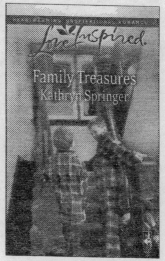

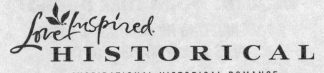

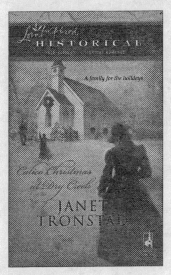

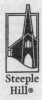